Burn Loeffke

From Warrior to Healer

*99 True Stories
from a General to his Children*

The Pacific Institute

Warrior to Healer

for Marc and Kristin,
and to the memory of Sgt. Larry Morford
4/8/48-2/12/70

Photographs on pages 8, 18, 32, 66, 76, 196
courtesy of the US Army

Images on pages 184 and 190 from C-SPAN,
used by permission

Contents

PART 3: SERVING IN PEACE TIME

PART 4: THE OLD RUSSIA

Part Five: CHINA

Part Six: THE MISSING

Part Seven: A FAREWELL AND NEW BEGINNING

REFLECTIONS

He worked us harder than any prior commander, but he was without a doubt the bravest individual I have ever met. Many of us initially thought Loeffke was too aggressive—the true 'war lover' soldier. We later saw him as a sensitive man dedicated to doing what he thought he should. At times I was convinced he was equally as dedicated to getting me killed. Regardless, I respect him as the finest leader I have ever known.

—Lee Lanning, **The Only War We Had**, New York: Ivy Books, 1987, p. 167

*

I am grateful to West Point for providing a compass on how to serve selflessly. West Point taught us discipline tempered with civility, and to say "No excuse, sir," holding us solely accountable for our own actions.

High praise is due Lee Lanning for chronicling our unit in combat. The Third Infantry Regiment is the President's Guard of Honor, and it was our privilege to command in that unit in battle.

My friends Lou and Diane Tice actively encouraged me to write this book and helped make its publication possible. They are outstanding models for how to serve a community. My appreciation to David Hills, a talented artist and good friend, and to Joyce Quick, a patient, skillful writer/editor, who stood by this project through draft after draft. To Dawn for making me smile again. This book has benefited from the design and typesetting of Hayes McNeill of M&M Scriveners.

Credit goes to Marc and Kristin's mother for bringing two beautiful children into this world, and to their grandparents, Hermann and Mother A, for being powerful positive influences.

Finally, my gratitude to the soldiers with whom I served our Country. May these stories commemorate their service.

FOREWORD

Burn Loeffke is an American hero who has lived life to the fullest. He has served his nation in war, peacemaking, and in reconciliation. He is both a warrior and a diplomat. In the latest chapter of his remarkable life, he has dedicated himself to the healing arts and to passing on what he has learned to his children and to all our children.

In these 99 stories he distills the lesson of life. He shares his darkest moments and his brightest. Above all, he shares the universal message of faith. Faith in one's self, faith in one's nation and faith in one's God.

Burn has been a friend of mine for 25 years. He has a generous spirit and it is as natural as breathing for him to dedicate this book and its proceeds to the memory of a fallen hero, Sgt. Larry Morford.

So read, enjoy, and be inspired by these stories and have your faith restored.

—Colin L. Powell
General, USA (Retired)

WARRIOR TO HEALER

These are stories that I would have sent to my children, had they been in the world when I was living most of these experiences. Too often, children grow up without ever really knowing their fathers, who are off somewhere making a living. My career in the military took me farther away for longer than most. Fortunately, my children and I have the gift of time together while they are still young. I put this book into print so that I can share this part of my life with them and with others, especially young people, who may be interested.

My generation became warriors when it fell upon us to fight our country's wars in foreign lands. The world has changed considerably since we fought these wars; unfortunately, Plato's warning that "Only the dead have seen the end of war," still holds true. The need for soldiers and heroes continues.

Yes, heroes. Today, the word may sound a bit old fashioned without the prefix "super," a superlative that serves only to diminish. Superheroes are comic book figures, and the closest they come to life is in the movies. Flesh and blood heroes, on the other hand, don't wear a badge announcing themselves, but you can't fail to notice them because they are so outstanding, so selflessly there for the other guy. Michael Blankfort, a biographer, says this about the substance of heroes: "Few men are won by principles alone, but rather by other men who preach them and live them. We are not followers of the word as much as we are of the deed which emerges from it. It was the example of Christ, not merely his sermons, which conquered his followers."

I once knew an incredible young man who preached and lived good deeds. His name was Larry Morford, and he was a soldier in the unit I commanded in Vietnam. I will never forget a conversation we once had. Larry said he didn't believe in war. He hated the very idea of it. When I asked why, if he felt this way, he had volunteered for combat duty, he said, "Sir, the job you and I are doing is a job of a beast and the least beastly of us should be doing it."

That was Larry's sermon, and he backed it up with action. He volunteered for every difficult and dangerous assignment. He just couldn't sit safely at home while other young men were being sent into combat. But he hated the senseless killing, the bloodshed, the barbarism of armed combat. He would sometimes ask me things like, "Why do we have to have night ambush patrols that kill instead of capture?" Sgt. Larry Morford was killed leading a night patrol 15 days before he was to return home. He was 22 years old.

Larry was just a sergeant in the U.S. Army who died, like so many others, in the jungles of Vietnam. Larry was also an extraordinary leader in the Army of the Lord. He influences me to this day. His impact has been greater than that of any other person I've ever met. Larry Morford was a hero, yet who has heard of him? That's the way it is with most real heroes. They don't get their pictures in the paper. They do their good works out of the sight of cameras, wherever it's needed. I hope these stories would have pleased him. And I hope my children grow up to be like him.

Part One:

CREATING A WARRIOR

1. Learning to Lead

I've heard it said that education is what we remember after we have forgotten the facts. Now, nearly 40 years later, I have forgotten most of the facts I learned at West Point. I can't remember much about nuclear physics, thermodynamics or electrical engineering. But I vividly remember the advice of an uncommonly wise sergeant: "Your soldiers won't care what you know until they know that you care. When they're convinced that you truly care, they'll follow you to hell and back."

As an officer, you show that you care when you are always last through the chow line. You show that you care when you are willing to listen and to endure the same hardships you ask your people to endure. Ultimately, you show that you care when you understand that you are there to serve those you command. You won't be able to do that unless they accept you as their leader, not because they have to obey you because of your rank, but because they trust and respect you.

It's no easy task to earn the respect and trust of those you are assigned to lead. They were in the unit before you arrived. Many have been in combat, felt the pain of wounds and tasted the sweat of intense fear. If it's your first command, you'll be seen as "green." So what does it take? The words of a sergeant come to mind: "We won't mind the cold if you shiver with us or the heat if you sweat with us." Your rank or title will mean little to most of the people you lead. It's your character that makes them want to follow you. And if your character is such that you are finally accepted by your soldiers, don't expect a celebration. If you're lucky, you might occasionally hear a simple comment that "You're all right."

At its best, the military is an environment in which we learn that we are more than we thought we were, can do more than we thought we could. Physical conditioning and courage are crucial ingredients, especially in combat. One of the greatest compliments that soldiers can bestow on a officer is their acknowledgment that "the old man can really hang in there."

"...and whoever would be first among you must be a slave of all." (Mark 10:44)

2. THE BOXING LESSON

All cadets had to box at West Point. The matches were chosen at random without regard to ability. I had never been inside a ring, and during my first fight I was knocked down hard several times. Afterward, I complained that it was an unfair battle, as my opponent was far more experienced. My instructor replied curtly, "Mister, you didn't learn your lesson." When I asked what that lesson might be, he answered: "In combat you don't get to choose your opponent."

The same is true in business, where we don't get to select our competitors, in school, where we don't get to choose our teachers, and in many other aspects of life, as well. We can't always choose the situations or the environment within which we must function. But we can choose to constantly work at expanding our limits, strengthening our character, building our stamina and growing our ability to care about others and offer our absolute best, no matter how difficult the circumstances.

"Though a man go out to battle a thousand times against a thousand men, if he conquers himself he is the greatest conqueror." Buddha

3. Building Stamina Through Sports

General George C. Marshall explained the need for military leaders to have stamina this way: "You have to lead men in war by requiring more from the individual than he thinks he can do. You have to lead men in war by bringing them along to thoughts of what they should be expected to do. You have to inspire them when they are hungry and exhausted, desperately uncomfortable and in great danger; and only a man with the positive characteristics of leadership and the physical stamina that goes with it can function under those conditions."

General Douglas MacArthur, one of West Point's most distinguished graduates, wrote, "A soldier's first priority is to be physically fit." He knew that without strong, healthy bodies, our ability to lead is severely diminished. Upon the wall of one of the Academy's gymnasiums was emblazoned another of MacArthur's beliefs: "On the fields of friendly strife are sown the seeds that, on other days, on other fields, will bear the fruits of victory."

At West Point I learned how important it is to provide opportunities for "friendly strife" to warriors. Through fiercely competitive athletics, the warrior spirit is strengthened. Sports build a soldier's confidence, stamina and physical strength—qualities that are much needed in combat. Team sports are especially effective at revealing the importance of a well thought out, flexible strategy, knowledge of the opponent's (and one's own) strengths and weaknesses, clear goals and objectives and clearly defined roles for each member of the team. They also reveal the importance of esprit de corps, belief in the wisdom of the team's leaders, and belief in the capabilities of oneself and the other team members.

"He that wrestles with us strengthens our nerves and sharpens our skill. Our antagonist is our helper." (Edmund Burke)

PERIODIC TABLE
MEMORIZE
-TOMORROW-
8-8:30 NUCLEAR PHYSICS
8:30-900 THERMODYNAMICS
9-9:30 FLUID MECHANICS
9:30-10 DIFFERENTIAL CALC
10-10:30 MECHANICS OF SOLIDS
10:30-11 ATOMIC RADIATION
11-12 TEST ON ALL
OF THE ABOVE

4. Every Leader a Teacher

At West Point, the discipline was mental as well as physical. We used to say that we had examiners instead of instructors, since cadets were tested daily. I was not one of the best mathematics students that West Point has seen. In fact, all the hard sciences were difficult for me. To this day, instead of combat, my nightmares reflect my old fears of having to recite laws of thermodynamics or mechanics of fluid. Yet, looking back I can see that the mental discipline these subjects required gave me practice in clear, logical thinking under pressure.

In the Army, we learned from manuals and then taught soldiers what we had learned. Teaching what we knew to others required a different set of skills than learning it in the first place. As we became senior officers, we had to educate legislators about the continuing need for defense. Only an effective teacher can do this.

Our nation loves peace and is historically wary of things military. Within six months after the end of the Revolutionary War, the Continental Congress wrote, "standing armies in time of peace are inconsistent with principles of republican government and are dangerous to the liberties of a free people." It then disbanded the remnant of the Continental Army, reducing the number of troops from 700 regulars to 25 privates to guard the stores at Fort Pitt and 55 to guard the stores at West Point. No officer was permitted to remain in service above the rank of Captain.

Later, during debates on the constitution, a clause was offered that would have prohibited our new armed forces from exceeding 3,000 men. Washington said he would support the proposal if the author would accept an amendment that prohibited any invading army from exceeding 2,000. Washington was a very effective teacher.

The only memos I have fully understood are the ones I wrote myself.

5. EVERY LEADER A STUDENT

"No study is possible on the battlefield; one does there simply what one can, in order to apply what one knows. Therefore, in order to do even a little, one has already to know a great deal and know it well," said Marshal Foch of the French Army.

The profession of arms requires constant learning. It is criminal to go into combat unprepared. Negligence in war means needless loss of life. We must be like sponges. We have to learn from books, from experience, from anything and everything. Something we learn today may be what saves tomorrow.

I learned to fly so that I could become a better navigator on the ground. I became a medic so that I would get used to seeing and caring for wounds in combat. Most importantly of all, I saw the necessity to have superbly physically fit commanders, who could lead in times of great stress.

In 1940, General George Marshall testified in Congress: "I saw about twenty-seven of twenty-nine divisions in battle. There were more failures, more crushed careers of officers of considerable rank, which grew out of physical exhaustion more than any other one cause. One acquired judgment with the years, but lost the resiliency of tendons and muscles." "Leadership in the field," he reported, "depends to an important extent on one's legs, stomach, nervous system, and on one's ability to withstand hardships and lack of sleep and still be disposed energetically and aggressively to command men and to dominate men on the battlefield. In World War I, many men had to be relieved because their spirit—their tenacity of purpose, their power of leadership over tired men—was broken through physical fatigue. They became pessimistic."

"The effective leader has the mind of a sage in the body of a savage."
(Chinese proverb)

MACC-1   24 May 1957

REGIMENTAL COMMANDERS AWARDS OF PUNISHMENT
NUMBER   37

Awards of punishment made by the Regimental Commander in the casses referred to him for action during the period 17 May to 24 May are published for the information of all cadets:

Co. & Class	Cadet Rank	Name	Offense	Punishment
B-1 3	Pvt	Rogers, DH	Approx 15 min late returning from Saturday evening privileges 17 May. (Reworded)	8 Demerits 8 Punishments
C-1 3	Pvt	Renalds, HH	Exercising extremely poor judgement, ie, addressing and replying to a 1st Classman in an insubordinate manner, 7 May. (Reworded)	10 Demerits 14 Punishments
D-1 1	Sgt	Teale, WE	Sitting in parked car, North Dock, 2207, 18 May.	5 Demerits 5 Confinements
F-1 4	Pvt	Stockton, PD	Approx 5 min late, return Armed Forces Trip Form, 18 May. (2nd similar offense) (Reworded)	10 Demerits 14 Punishments
I-1 4	Pvt	Schannep, RN	Public display of affection toward young lady in Grand Central Station, NYC, approx 2400 hrs, 18 May.	10 Demerits 14 Punishments
K-1 2	Cpl	Ward, WW	Judgement, not exercising proper; ie, voicing disagreement with officer instructor in presence of class in such a manner and tone of voice as to indicate disgust and disrespect during critique of an unsatisfactory MIT presentation, 11 May.	10 Demerits 14 Confinements
M-1 4	Pvt	Brennan, AW	Gross indifference to the 4th Class System as evidenced by failure to respond to specific corrections, failure to obey specific orders, and receiving twenty Fourth Class Delinquency Reports in 28 days, 21 May.	15 Demerits 20 Punishments

FOR THE COMMANDER:

OFFICIAL:

T. H. MONROE, JR.
Lt. Colonel, Infantry
Executive Officer

14

6. Who Makes General?

Making General should not be an officer's dream. Very few make it. Over 700 young men entered West Point along with me in 1953. Four years later, 540 graduated. Of that number, fewer than 40 of us were promoted to Generals. Only one of our classmates, Carl Vuono, became Chief of Staff. Those of us who made it worked hard, had good bosses, and were lucky that we didn't get killed. We were seen by the right people at the right time—doing the right thing. If I were to name the ingredients necessary to be successful in the Military, they would be luck, experience, courage, caring, hard work, and more luck.

Clausewitz taught that "Courage is the soldier's first requirement." He went on to add, "A strong will is a must. In combat, as each man's strength gives out, as it no longer responds to his will, the inertia of the whole gradually comes to rest on the commander's will alone. The ardor of his spirit must rekindle the flame of purpose in all others; his inward fire must revive their hope. Only to the extent that he can do this will he retain his hold on his men and keep control . . . .The burdens increase with the number of men in his command, and therefore, the higher his position, the greater the strength of character he needs to bear the mounting load."

One should enter the military to live an adventure and serve the nation. When I was young, I thought that being a doctor was the best profession, because you were in the business of saving lives. When I graduated from West Point, I believed that a good officer could save, through his decisions, more lives than the average doctor. At the end of 35 years in the military, I was convinced of the truth of that statement.

Doing the right thing is important, but doing the right thing for the right reasons is even more important.

15

7. Getting Us Ready for Combat

After graduation from West Point, we were sent to parachute school where we learned to conquer fear. Jumping out of an aircraft increases confidence and courage.

Next came ranger school. Ranger school taught us how far we could go and how much we could endure. We quickly discovered that we could do what seemed to be humanly impossible with only two or three hours sleep and little food. These two courses prepared us to lead in combat.

I then reported to the 82nd Parachute Division, but the tour was short-lived. Special Forces were looking for officers who could speak French. I volunteered, and was accepted. Knowledge of languages would become important in my career. I was the first of my class-mates to taste combat simply because I spoke French.

"Airborne!" (paratrooper greeting) means that if you ask me to go a mile, I will give you two.

8. Fear of Fear: My First Jump

Those who have never engaged in dangerous activities, often ask, "How can fear be conquered?"

My first parachute jump is a good example of how we dealt with fear. We had just finished ground training, and we were waiting to board our airplanes for our first parachute jumps. The head parachute instructor yelled over the loudspeaker, "This will be the last time you will get the opportunity to refuse to jump before we board the airplanes. We don't want to have to deal with refusals inside the planes. If you are going to quit, do it now!"

Eleven soldiers stepped forward. I gulped and said to myself, "Maybe it takes more courage to refuse and be paraded in front of five-hundred of us than just to go ahead and jump." I jumped. General Patton used to say, "We have to train our people so that they will act courageously out of fear of showing fear." In the sixth century B.C., the Greek poet/philosopher Homer said, "Do the thing you fear." That's how you conquer it. As the Nike ads proclaim, "Just do it!"

Courage isn't the absence of fear. Courage is being afraid and doing what we need to do anyway.

9. A World Record Broken

The most demanding school I ever attended was the U.S. Army's Ranger School. This school's two and one-half months of "hell" prepared us for combat. We were chased by military dogs, went three days without food, and moved over the worst terrain in the worst weather. The motto "Rangers lead the way" is legendary. In my days, the Army

THE ACTION

wanted to place at least one Ranger soldier per each forty-men unit. The Ranger-trained soldier and officer would provide the backbone for our combat units.

I remember the anguish of being lost in the jungle because we failed to navigate properly. This mistake made us walk through horrible terrain for twenty miles more than we needed to. This taught me that what soldiers want most from their officers is that they listen to them and not get them lost or killed.

Two events stand out from our experience in Ranger School. We were so tired from moving day and night, with only a couple of hours of sleep, that when we halted for five minutes, we were not allowed to sit or we would fall asleep and be left behind. One night, a classmate sat down anyway. Suddenly he felt warm liquid dripping down his face. He was so beat, he could only manage a weak request: "Could you pee a little more to the left?"

The second event dealt with Ranger School's desire to get us over the fear of snakes and alligators. I remember walking through swamps very slowly, watching water moccasins moving away from our paths. Earlier in the course, they had tried to convince us that we could distract alligators by making noise. For me, alligators proved to be a nightmare.

I had been selected to swim the rope across rivers and streams. This was a dubious distinction I received when a classmate told our group that I was a good swimmer. Some of the men would go up and down river and splash the water, hoping to distract the critters, while I swam with a rope tied around my waist. When I reached the other side, I would tie my end of the rope high on a tree so that the rest of the patrol could hand-walk across it, without touching the water. The next to last day that we were in the swamps, I was swimming the rope across when I heard a splash and someone yell, "Alligator, alligator!" I swam the rest of the distance in world record time!

We'll never know what we can do until we have a powerful motivator. Sometimes it will be fear, sometimes love.

10. LANGUAGES OPEN DOORS

When I was a young lieutenant, I was asked to report to General Stilwell, who had the reputation of eating young officers for breakfast. Stilwell was, at the time, Chief of Staff of our Parachute Corps, a position I would assume some twenty years later. He asked that I translate his remarks into Portuguese for a group of officers from the Brazilian War College.

My efforts to interpret his speech were Herculean, but fell short of what was required. I had not looked at a Portuguese book or spoken the language since I had left West Point. Stilwell spoke for a long time, making it difficult to remember everything he said, and I know I left out several points. The General ended his presentation with a humorous anecdote. I told the Brazilian officers that I did not know how to translate his joke and respectfully requested that they laugh anyway. The Brazilians roared and General Stilwell was satisfied that the talk had been well received. As a result, I felt my promotion to Captain was assured.

From this experience, I learned the importance of using expert interpreters, since they may change what is actually meant in their translation efforts. Someone needs to verify the competency and fluency of the interpreter. Better yet, don't depend on translation. Learn the language. Sharing a common language opens the doors to friendship.

We will not be accepted because of our ability to speak a foreign language as much as our ability to express love.

11. Parachuting with Dynamite

I was assigned to a demolition team where we practiced parachuting from high altitudes with explosives. One day, I didn't properly adjust my pack to my parachute harness, and when I opened my chute at the prescribed altitude, the bag with the explosives was ripped from my harness and plummeted down some 500 feet. Luckily, no damage was done to anything but my pride. This taught me the necessity of checking and double-checking equipment before operations.

In Vietnam, our enemy never attacked without five rehearsals. In our unit, we had three. The first was done in slow motion; the second was at regular speed, but without all our equipment; and the third was done fully equipped at regular speed.

He who prepares well, wins well.

PART TWO:

ONE PLACE, THREE WARS

12. The First War

We were enjoying the glamour that comes from being in the Army's Special Forces. We were double volunteers, for parachute duty and Special Forces. The concept of Special Forces was that ten soldiers and two officers could train, equip and lead in combat operations, if need be, five hundred irregulars. Most of us were also Rangers, and wearing green berets was a sign of prestige. We were special. We had all signed up to jump behind enemy lines, if necessary.

One day, I received a message to report to a briefing room. There were more than 40 men in the room, and the mood was tense. Our Colonel stood up and said, "Gentlemen, you have been chosen for a sensitive mission. Let me remind you of the paper you signed about volunteering to work behind enemy lines. If there are any of you who have reservations about accepting this assignment, I do not want to see you in this room when I resume my briefing in twenty minutes." Whereupon, the Colonel departed. When he returned twenty minutes later, the room had three fewer men. I later found out that those three had been asked to leave Special Forces that same day.

We remained at Fort Bragg in isolation for several days. We went through intensive briefings and training. Then we were on our way overseas. No one would hear from me for the next few months.

This was a period of a vacuum of power in Southeast Asia. The French had just been defeated and anti-Communist governments needed help to survive. During that year, I experienced what real fear was.

Happiness more often comes from needing few things than from accumulating many. The so-called primitive people we trained were happier than many wealthy Americans I knew.

13. MY FAVORITE BLONDE

As a young Lieutenant with no experience of married life or even a prolonged relationship with a woman, the idea of dying was hard to accept. I prayed that I'd be spared so I could enjoy a wife and family before my life ended.

This longing kept returning. I felt cheated. Thoughts of death and a too-soon interrupted life kept swimming in my head. Add to that the lack of mail—no warm words from anyone we knew, because, officially, we weren't here. Our mission was classified, so we would receive no mail for the duration.

To keep up our morale, the First Sergeant had asked us, before we deployed, to check off the type of woman we wanted to write to us. I selected blonde, with interests in sports, music and languages. Every month, I would receive a letter (from the First Sergeant), signed "From your sporty blonde, who misses her brave soldier tremendously!"

Being remembered provides comfort.

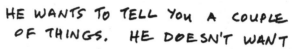

HE WANTS TO TELL YOU A COUPLE OF THINGS. HE DOESN'T WANT TO DIE WITHOUT CONFESSING HIS SINS.

14. BLESS ME, FATHER

"Mon Père, il veut vous dire quelque chose. Il veut pas mourir avant de parler avec vous." Father, he wants to tell you some things. He doesn't want to die before he speaks with you. He wants to confess his sins and ask forgiveness.

One of my duties in Special Forces in Southeast Asia was to assist in interpreting French. Before deploying to a sensitive area, several of the men who were Catholics wanted their confessions heard. The only priests available who were cleared were French. I became a middleman for confessions.

In war, many of us become religious. We want to feel closer to God. The ever-present possibility of dying is a constant reminder to put our affairs in order.

"To have faith is to be sure of the things we hope for, to be certain of the things we cannot see." (Hebrews 11:1)

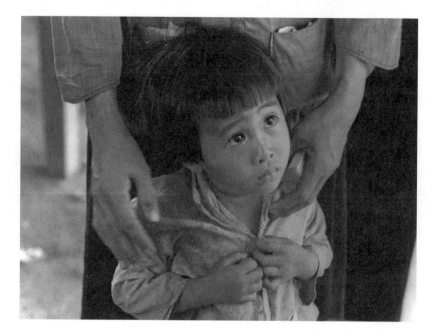

15. HEAL FIRST

Special Forces taught me how to be accepted in foreign lands. In trying to gain the confidence and trust of strangers, three skills proved valuable. The first of these is healing.

Healing is especially effective when dealing with those whom we call primitive. Many of them treat healers like gods. Wherever we went, one of our first activities was to set up a dispensary to treat the illnesses and heal those whom we would have to advise or befriend. Once we had gained their trust and confidence, they were willing to do what we asked of them.

It was during this tour that I saw firsthand the effectiveness of preaching by first healing. I saw our hosts learn to love the missionaries as they experienced their selflessness. Then they soon began to ask about the God these healers prayed to. But it was the healing that first sparked their interest. They wanted to know more about this God who was even greater than the people who had just repaired their broken bodies.

"Preach . . . if you must use words." (Unknown)

16. Shall We Sing?

The second skill that proved valuable in being accepted in foreign lands was music. As in almost any group, some of us played musical instruments and some of us sang. At night, we would gather around and play tunes, often on a harmonica. The natives would listen attentively. We would then make sounds that they could echo, and soon we had an enthusiastic chorus.

Years later, I learned that music could also help us teach and learn languages more rapidly. Moreover, it has been demonstrated that those who have had strokes can relearn speech more rapidly by singing. Music reaches our soul. It affects both the so-called primitive and the most sophisticated. It lifts morale and lightens the spirit. That is why armies have bands.

Training our hosts to fight was not difficult. They were already warriors. What we needed to do was teach them the techniques of using modern weapons. By befriending them with healing, music, laughter, we were able to train a fair size force in a relatively short time.

Healing + Music + Laughter = Friendship

17. Laughter and Magic

The third skill that proved valuable in winning the confidence and friendship of our foreign hosts worked, literally, like magic. We learned to perform magic tricks for their amusement. One that never failed to entertain involved three sticks. One had a rattle in it. The object of the game was to guess which one. We would pick one of the sticks that didn't rattle, show it to everyone, and make it rattle. We did this by means of a rattle hidden between the fingers of the demonstrator. When the stick was returned to the table and moved around slowly, the audience thought they could easily follow its movements. A volunteer chosen by the group would then point out the stick they all "knew" was the one with the rattle. But, of course, he was always wrong! This went on, night after night, while the natives laughed uproariously when their representative chose the "wrong" stick.

The laughter and applause generated by this and other simple illusions convinced me to learn a few tricks I could use in any situation. They have served me well on many occasions. I have taught my children how to work these tricks, and my son, Marc, used them in 1994 to entertain children during our 500 kilometer run in Argentina.

Live swiftly and kindly and...make them laugh.

18. FRIENDS UNTIL WHEN?

This war convinced me that we should not volunteer to assist others if we are not serious about the durability of our offer. As a young lieutenant, I saw U.S. troops pulling out from a base camp that was about to be overrun because Americans were not to be captured. We boarded the aircraft, under direct orders, and left our friends behind to fend for themselves. I can still see their faces as they watched us walking away as the attackers were closing in. We would repeat this same action 12 years later in Saigon. These two episodes hardened my conviction that the United States should not commit itself to something it couldn't see through.

Our political leaders need to be educated about what it means to fight a ground war. Our competitors had much experience in fighting foreigners. Marshal Tran Hung Dao, the Vietnamese General who defeated the Mongols almost 700 years ago, described his strategy this way:

> *We must weaken him by drawing him into prolonged campaigns. Once his initial dash is broken, it will be easier to destroy him. . . . When the enemy is away from home for a long time and produces no victories and families learn of their dead, then the enemy population at home becomes dissatisfied and considers it a mandate from heaven that the armies be recalled. Time is always in our favor. Our climate, mountains and jungles discourage the enemy; but for us they offer both sanctuary and a place from which to attack.*

This successful strategy, seven centuries old, worked against us in the 1970s.

"When we are needed, we'll be there..." (U.S. Army song)

Volume 11, N° 19 SAIGON, VIET NAM SEPTEMBER 14. 1963

Heavy VC Losses In Major Encounters

A fierce major battle — called by one observer "possibly the biggest engagement since April erupted Tuesday in An Xuyen province on the Camau peninsula on the southern tip of Viet Nam.

Earliest reports from the battlefield Wednesday morning stated that the Viet Cong had suffered at least 120 killed in the first day's action.

Heliborne Vietnamese Marines clashed initially with the communists near the town of Dam Doi which the VC had earlier captured

and occupied. The enemy suffered 30 dead in the first battle. Later, a large scale 'five hour fire fight developed, with resulting VC casualties reported as "at least" 122 killed.

Before dark Tuesday, Large elements of the Vietnamese Airborne Brigade were drooped by C-47s and USAF 123s near the town of Cai Nuoc, about 15 miles west of Dam Doi.

Concentrated air strikes hammered Viet Cong positions. Fragmentary Air Force reports claimed many enemy killed from the air but it was not determined by press time whether or not this claim was in addition to, or included with the 122 dead reported in the Marine clash.

19. The Second War

My second war in Southeast Asia was as an advisor to a Vietnamese parachute unit. It was a strange experience. We fought intensely for a couple of days and then were free to swim and play tennis in Saigon. Most of the blood was being shed by the Vietnamese. We assisted by calling in air strikes, evacuating the injured, adjusting artillery, and making sure supplies were delivered.

We also experimented with new techniques. One of these was called Eagle Flight. The idea was to use a helicopter flying at low altitudes to attract fire. As soon as fire was received, the enemy position was radioed and troops in other helicopters would assault that position. We did this successfully for months. Then, the enemy learned our tactics, and our casualties increased.

This began the education of U.S. officers in the handling of large units in combat. It helped me learn how to fight from the air.

Isolated outposts need to believe they will be reinforced if they will hold out until help arrives. Our policy was to reinforce any unit within 24 hours after it reported being attacked. A defender, therefore, knew that if he could hang on for 24 hours, help would arrive.

We had units that slept under the wings of transport aircraft, waiting for the word to go into combat. Parachute operations validated the importance of providing hope to units that were surrounded and alone. This second war emphasized air power. We could not get to our objective without the Air Force, and, once there, we were usually outside the range of friendly artillery.

Vietnamese paratroopers made many combat parachute jumps. Their battle drills were simple and well executed. After a jump, we would always reorganize, with Alpha Company to the north, Bravo to the east, Charlie to the south, and Delta to the west.

Some will fight, even in hopeless situations. For most of us, to know that help is coming strengthens our resolve to continue the struggle.

20. WHITE CAN BE DANGEROUS

The first day of my second war was a long one. I was deposited on top of a hill by a helicopter that was under fire the last 400 meters into the area. Then I was rushed off to the battalion commander for a briefing.

The unit had been in the area for 15 days and had encountered enemy in almost every direction. We were surrounded. The battalion was waiting for a Marine Corps unit to get within two or three kilometers before trying to push out from the hilltop. We would wait for it ten more days, all the while patrolling aggressively to keep the enemy from firing into our inner perimeter.

The first night, I was awakened when mortar rounds started coming in. I dropped out of my hammock into a shallow hole that was full of rain water. As the rounds continued, I decided to make a dash for the command post, which I knew had overhead cover. As I was running, literally for my life, I felt small arms fire hitting close by. I jumped into the trench surrounding the command post and crawled inside. The battalion commander and the operations officer were calling for artillery. The commander looked up and said, "You were lucky you weren't killed because of that shirt. White makes a beautiful target at night for enemy snipers." I learned that the enemy would crawl close to the perimeter, under the protection of their mortars, and shoot at anything that moved. I discarded all my white T-shirts and traded C-rations and a compass for some Vietnamese shirts. It wasn't until the mid-1960s that the U.S. Army finally changed from white to gray T-shirts.

Those ten days convinced me that the best protection against mortars and artillery was to be well dug in. Units that did not dig in suffered casualties when attacked by small arms and indirect fires. Our deep trenches saved us from the nightly shelling.

Learning from others who have more experience is wisdom.

USAF-TRANSPORTED AIRBORNE BRIGADE
Dropping into a Viet Cong stronghold from C-123s.

21. A Different Weapon for a Different Fight

I learned many new lessons in my second combat experience. For example, never carry two weapons that use different ammunition. I went into combat with a carbine (for firing at medium range) and a .45 caliber pistol (for close range protection). Once, after we had been in a long firefight, I ran out of ammunition for my carbine and found the .45 useless for anything over 15 meters away. What I needed was ammo for my carbine. From then on, I carried a rifle and grenades and gave away the pistol.

I learned that different weapons are needed for different terrain. Our parachute units deployed wherever there was trouble. It was not uncommon for us to be fighting one week in the open spaces of the southern part of South Vietnam and the next week in dense jungle near the northern part.

Whenever we knew we were going into dense jungle, we parachuted with Thompson submachine guns. In this type of vegetation, we could not see the enemy, but we could hear the whine of his bullets coming toward us. The best way to respond is a heavy volume of saturation fire with a weapon like the Thompson. When we fought in areas where the visibility was better than 15 or 20 meters, we used the M1 rifle with its long-range capability. The M1 fire was accurate, so most of the time we fired single rounds. I was now becoming an experienced warrior.

Experience may not always be the most important factor, but I cannot recall when it has not been.

22. My First Jump into Combat

I made two combat jumps in the 1960s. The first was into an area that was flooded and experiencing heavy winds. We were receiving ground fire as we exited the aircraft. Our casualties, however, all came from excessive winds and drownings. The strong winds wouldn't allow me to collapse my chute. It was the monsoon season, and I kept skidding through the paddy fields and slamming into dikes. Some of the soldiers who were killed were knocked unconscious when they slammed into dikes and then drowned. We looked like we were water-skiing behind our parachutes.

This combat jump was costly in equipment, as well. Trying to get out of my chute, I lost my weapon, binoculars, helmet, compass, and canteen. Several mortars, heavy machine-guns, recoilless rifles, and radios were lost in the flooded paddies. It took us the better part of two hours to start moving toward the objective. The only paratrooper who grappled with the enemy was the commander's cook. Landing on top of a sampan, he captured one enemy soldier and killed another.

Even the best planned operation may be a disaster if the weather does not cooperate.

23. DUCKS MAKE GOOD SOLDIERS

During my first tour in Vietnam, the Air Force would drop, by parachute, boxes full of live chickens and ducks. Vietnamese troops would place these animals out on the perimeter as guards. They were excellent security. Ducks, especially, would alert at the slightest movement in their vicinity. As our food supply dwindled, we would eat the ducks and chickens. The Vietnamese soldier would march with a live chicken or duck inside his backpack. It made for an interesting sight, duck heads sticking out of a long row of packs.

History tells us that Roman Legions also used geese to warn them of intruders. We have forgotten many useful history lessons and spent billions on technology, where in some instances, security and nourishment can be provided with just a few quackers.

Sometimes simple is best and often less expensive.

THE SAIGON POST

Nº 59   Thursday, March 5, 1964   TEN PIASTERS

WOUNDED PARATROOP COMMANDER
REFUSES TO LEAVE TROOPS

Major Gen. Nguyen Khanh, MRC Chairman and Prime Minister, pins the two silver stars of a brigadier general to the V.N. Army on Airborne Brigade Commander Cao Van Vien, at the new general's bedside at the Cong Hoa Military Hospital yesterday. Gen. Khanh, accompanied by Maj. Gen. Tran Thien Khiem, Commander-in-chief of the VN Armed Forces and Defense Minister and Brig. Gen. Lam Van Phat, Commander of Army Corps III, also visited other soldiers wounded in Tuesday's battle of Kien Phong.

130 Rebels Killed; Airborne Brigade Chief Wounded

Vietnamese paratroopers Tuesday morning foiled an important top-level conference of Viet Cong commanders at the cost of heavy casualties, ARVN sources revealed yesterday. Two crack Viet Cong battalions assigned to provide security for the meeting withdrew into Cambodia after a bloody three-hour battle in muddy Kien Phong province with the airborne troops dropped barely 2,000 yards from the border.

Col. Cao Van Vien, commander of the Airborne Brigade, himself got a bullet through the shoulder early in the morning when an airborne battalion he was leading was ambushed by well-concealed Viet Cong heavy-weapons units. He was decorated by the MRC Chairman, Gen. Nguyen Khanh, at the Cong Hoa Hospital yesterday morning and given the two stars of a Brigadier General.

Vien was the highest-ranking Vietnamese commander to be hit in battle in years. His condition was described by doctors as not serious.

An American captain was among the 19 killed in the operation. It was officially reported that the government forces had 55 wounded.

According to ARVN sources, the important Viet Cong conference was believed scheduled in preparation for the forthcoming visit here by U.S. Defense Secretary McNamara and the U.S. JCS Chief, Gen. Maxwell D. Taylor.

The sources said that an estimated 130 Viet Cong were killed on the semi-flooded battlefield. Around 85 of these were believed killed by air strikes. The guerrillas gave up the fight and retreated across the Cambodian border shortly before noon Tuesday.

The battle was described by a U.S. military adviser as the fiercest fight I've seen since World War II.

The shooting began when an airborne battalion was negotiating a wide canal running into the Mekong River when it enters Vietnamese territory from Cambodia. The Viet Cong opened up first on the exposed flank of the paratrooper columns as it began to cross over.

A savage barrage of automatic arms fire and a hail of shells from branch mortars and recoilless rifles [...]

24. My Wounded Go First

Our Vietnamese unit was ordered to parachute near the Cambodian border, where intelligence suspected the location of a headquarters. Within minutes after the jump, our unit was ambushed and suffered heavy casualties.

Help would not be forthcoming. No support or fire were allowed within five miles of the international border. Nevertheless, the unit managed to save itself, largely through the heroic action of its Commander, Colonel Cao Van Vien. Vien had been wounded in the initial minutes of the ambush. Although in considerable pain, he kept his head and saw that the only way to save the unit would be to assault. He led the charge, routed the enemy, and then refused to be evacuated until all his wounded had gotten out. Legends are created about such heroes.

"One man with courage makes a majority." (Andrew Jackson)

25. Lost

The plea of a soldier to his lieutenant: "Sir, please don't get us lost!" During many of the assaults that we conducted, it was not uncommon to be lost. Almost every time we went somewhere, the area was unfamiliar—a new place with different vegetation. I would know basically where I was going from having studied a map, but we often circled in different directions, and it was easy to lose our bearings. I swore that for the next war I would be better prepared to lead from the air, and decided to learn to fly.

After that second war, while attending the Armed Forces Staff College at Norfolk, Virginia, I would take off after school and fly. Flying taught me radio-telephone procedures, the importance of weather, and how to navigate and orient myself in unfamiliar terrain. I also learned the capabilities and limitations of aircraft. I could now ask pilots to do things they had previously told me they could not do.

Flying teaches valuable skills. Most of the time during a battle, soldiers will not see their commander, but can hear his voice. A clear voice instills confidence, and pilots are experienced radio operators. The more we use the radio, the more confident we sound. When we fly, we are constantly on the radio talking to a tower or to a radar controller asking for directions, weather reports, or requesting landing instructions.

"The world is a place no one yet ever knew by description; one must travel it oneself to be acquainted with it." (Lord Chesterfield)

26. The Third War

During the late '60s, we fought with U.S. troops who were mainly draftees. The infantry battalion I commanded was more than 96 percent draftee. The majority proved to be good soldiers. Many, however, did not want to be in the Army, much less in Vietnam. A slogan at that time was, "Hell no, we won't go!" In the U.S., many refused to be drafted. In Vietnam, our jails were overflowing with soldiers who would not go into combat. One soldier captured a common attitude by saying, "What's two years in jail compared to dying?"

Another challenge was that many of the professional sergeants who had been in Vietnam in the early 1960s were no longer in our combat units. Many had been wounded or killed, or had transferred to less dangerous specialties. As a result, this war was fought with junior leaders—draftees who had been promoted in combat.

I remember being criticized for not being at my command post. Finally, I convinced my brigade commander that this war was mainly a small-unit war. Battalion Commanders needed to know personally the conditions existing where the soldiers fought.

I spent most of my time in the forward companies with my artillery fire support coordinator and a communicator. A company was almost always in combat, and I wanted to be with that unit. In the evenings, I would join patrols. During the first week after I took over the command, I found poor noise discipline and widespread snoring. Patrols had an excessive number of personnel. Equipment was not tightly tied down, rehearsals were not conducted, claymores were badly located. In short, it was a disaster. The truth of the well-known statement that "the unit does well only what the commander checks" was proven to me.

I accompanied at least three night patrols a week. This forced lieutenants and captains to frequently go on night ambushes. The number of soldiers in a patrol was no more than 15. This put everyone on alert, as they knew this size force could not survive a surprise attack.

"This is courage in a man: To bear unflinchingly what heaven sends."
(Euripides)

27. Tennis, Anyone?

Colonel Bobby Gard and I were playing tennis in a southern city of Vietnam, when enemy mortar fire started to hit our positions. The Colonel was an avid tennis player, but, on this day, I was winning by one game. When I suggested stopping because the mortar fire was coming dangerously close, he smiled slightly and said, "We're not quitting until this score changes."

I offered to proclaim him the winner if we could get off the court and go to the bunkers where we'd be safe. He wouldn't hear of it. This tournament would determine the winner of the tennis competition. So we kept on playing. I definitely did not think winning a game was worth losing our lives. All I wanted was to get out of there. I made sure he won the next points. We declared him the winner and ran the 200 or so meters to the safety of the bunkers.

———————————

At times, the better part of valor is to live to play or fight another day.

DEPARTMENT OF THE ARMY
HEADQUARTERS 9TH INFANTRY DIVISION
APO San Francisco 96370

GENERAL ORDERS
NUMBER   7317   24 June 1969

AWARD OF THE SILVER STAR

1. TC 320. The following AWARD is announced.

LOEFFKE, BERNARD 078088 (SSAN: 054-32-9568) MAJOR, INFANTRY,
United States Army, Headquarters and Headquarters Company,
9th Infantry Division APO 96370
Awarded: Silver Star (1st Oak Leaf Cluster)
Date action: 11 June 1969
Theater: Republic of Vietnam
Reason: For gallantry in action involving close combat with an armed hostile force in th
          Republic of Vietnam: Major Loeffke distinguished himself by exceptionally valoro
          actions on 11 June 1969 while serving as Assistant Chief of Staff, G5, 9th Infan
          Division. While traveling south on the road between Highway 4 and Dong Tam, Maj
          Loeffke arrived on the scene of an enemy ambush against a truck convoy. Although
          heavy enemy sniper fire was still being received, he courageously rushed to the
          aid of a soldier who had been seriously wounded during the initial stages of the
          attack. Realizing the casualty needed to reach a medical facility quickly,
          Major Loeffke carried the man to his jeep and travelled on through the killing
          zone of the enemy ambush to evacuate the soldier to the hospital at Dong Tam.
          Major Loeffke's extraordinary heroism in close combat with an armed hostile for
          is in keeping with the highest traditions of the military service and reflects
          great credit upon himself, the 9th Infantry Division and the United States Army.
Authority: By direction of the President under the provisions of the Act of Congress,
          approved 9 July 1918, and USARV message 16695, dated 1 July 1966.

FOR THE COMMANDER:

OFFICIAL: R. G. GARD, JR.
                                                  COL, GS
                                                  Chief of Staff

ROBERT A. JOHNSON
MAJ, AGC
Adjutant General

DISTRIBUTION: SPECIAL DISTRIBUTION:
  5-ea indiv conc   2-TAGO DA ATTN: AGPF-F
  1-ea indiv 201 file   (for official personnel file)
  2-PIO   2-Dir, OPD, OPO, DA ATTN: OPIN
  2-AVDE-MH (19thMHD)
  2-CG USARV ATTN: AVHAG-DB   28-Total
  2-HHC, 9th Inf. Div.
  10-Ch Awds & Dec.

58

28. Whose Blood?

While driving back from Saigon one day, we encountered a long column of vehicles that had stopped and were blocking traffic. A sergeant was not allowing anyone to proceed. He informed us that the lead vehicles of the convoy had been ambushed. I asked if there were any casualties. He said he thought there were several dead and wounded, and that enemy snipers were everywhere. I went forward as far as I could and saw a soldier moving beside a damaged truck some 100 yards away. I placed a couple of soldiers into positions and asked them to start firing into both sides of the brush. I told my driver to get out of the jeep and then drove as fast as I could past the wounded soldier and jumped into a trench and started to work my way back to the wounded man.

Bullets were now coming from both sides of the road. When I reached him, I could see that the soldier had a chest wound and both legs had been shattered. He was delirious and unable to move or speak. I tried a fireman's carry. I made about 15 yards when snipers zeroed in on us and put another bullet into the wounded man's right leg. I crawled the next 20 yards pulling him towards the jeep. By then, another of our jeeps with a machine gun appeared on the other side of the road and started firing into the brush. I used the covering fire to stand up and carry him the last few yards. His blood was all over me. I couldn't tell which was his blood and which was mine, since I had received a minor wound to the hand.

I managed to get him to the field hospital and later found out that he lived, but he lost both legs.

Sometimes, we act without fear when we see others in pain.

29. THE FOXHOLE EXCHANGE PROGRAM

To increase the morale of our soldiers, we devised the Foxhole Exchange Program. A company commander would identify the best soldier in his unit, and I would send him back to sleep in my tent, while I replaced him in his unit. This allowed me to observe and feel what our soldiers were experiencing. The exchange program was a great morale booster, as all the soldiers wanted to sleep in my tent and eat hot meals in the rear. It didn't work miracles, but it was appreciated. I remember one letter in particular:

Dear Colonel,

I thank you for letting me exchange places with you. The men also appreciate what you are doing. However, I still don't like the Army, and I still don't like officers. As a matter of fact, my favorite prayer goes this way: "O Lord, distribute bullets as you do the pay; let the officers get most of them."

Respectfully,
Citizen Jenkins

"Everything I did in my life that was worthwhile, I caught hell for."
—Chief Justice Earl Warren

30. HANDKERCHIEFS! NO HANDKERCHIEFS!

Sometimes our soldiers ridiculed Vietnamese customs and behaviors—for example, the way the Vietnamese blew their noses. They would press a nostril with one finger and blow the other. Some of our troops considered this a crude, uncivilized, dirty habit.

One day, I asked a Vietnamese friend to tell us how we were perceived. "Are you sure you want to know?" When I said, "Yes," he became excited and replied, "The farmers see you blowing your noses into a cloth and then packing that dirty cloth into your pocket and using it again. They call you 'dirt carriers.' They think their way is much more civilized, cleaner, and makes more sense. They don't have to wash a dirty cloth, and as you know, clean water is a precious commodity."

Sometimes something that doesn't "make sense" on the surface will reveal itself as perfectly sensible, once we have more information.

31. HERE WE ARE!

At one point, we discovered that our resupply procedures were giving away the location of our patrols. We learned from captured documents and prisoners that the enemy placed people in the tops of trees so they could see where the helicopters were dropping supplies or where they were landing. They then used this information to prepare ambushes.

One method of resupplying patrols that were sent out for long periods of time was through the use of caches. We would hide supplies in certain areas, then come back with patrols and use those supplies. To deceive the enemy, our helicopters would drop dummy resupplies (old newspapers and empty boxes) in five or six areas, hoping to lure the enemy away from the real drop. The helicopters would loiter at the dummy areas but would drop supplies quickly at our true location.

One problem we had to solve was how to signal our position to the helicopter without using smoke. We devised a sturdy balloon that we would push through the canopy until it was flush with the top of the trees. It could not be seen from the horizon, but a helicopter flying overhead could easily spot the location.

At times, deception may be the best tactic.

32. Too Much of a Good Thing

In Vietnam, we were fortunate to have an over-abundance of air assets. In fact, there was a standing order that if we came in contact with the enemy and didn't call for air support within five minutes, we would have to explain the reason in writing to our brigade commander.

But air support wasn't much help in dense jungle. To use it, we needed 500 meters separation from the target, and artillery had to be shut off while air support was being used.

In dense jungle, we normally made contact with the enemy no more than 5 to 20 meters away. We would then have to withdraw 500 meters. The enemy soon learned how to survive air strikes. They had a tactic called "Hug the belts of the Americans." As we withdrew, they advanced, because they knew that bombs were going to be dropped on them if they didn't.

Before the actual drop, we had to identify our front lines. We used smoke grenades to do this, but by the time the smoke went through the vegetation, it had drifted enough so that it wasn't an accurate marker. Plus, the smoke would give our positions away to the enemy. Nevertheless, we were literally carrying more smoke grenades than ammunition. Instead of smoke grenades, we decided to substitute the front of an M79 shell with tightly rolled engineer tape. When we fired this shell through the tops of the trees, the shell exploded, the tape unfurled, laying on top of the trees, and our position was marked accurately and discreetly.

To survive in tough competition, innovation is needed.

33. THREE PRAYERS

I felt myself changing during my three combat tours. The way I prayed reflected these changes.

My first experience was as a young Lieutenant with a Special Forces team in the middle of strangers in a foreign land. I prayed hard that I would return home safely. It was a selfish prayer.

In my second tour as a Captain, I fell in love with the courage and sacrifice of the Vietnamese paratroopers we were advising. I prayed for their safety as well as my own.

My third experience was as a combat Commander responsible for the lives of almost one thousand soldiers. Their safety largely depended on my training and experience, and the decisions I made. It was during this time that I changed most. These were my soldiers, these were my children. I found myself praying mainly for them. I felt every death and every wound personally. I was also praying for the badly wounded enemy that had just tried to kill me.

We are all God's children. We need to learn how to be a better family.

BZZZAW!
WHEEEE
BLUB BLUB BLUB
BZZZZZONK!
SNORT
QUICK! GET HIS GAS MASK!

34. SOMEONE IS SNORING

In any group of ten men, two to three will usually be snorers. We could not keep everyone awake in ambush patrols at night, because we marched long distances all day. During night patrols, we allowed some to sleep while others stayed on alert.But the noise from sleeping soldiers' snoring could get us all killed. We finally solved it, thanks to the suggestion of a young soldier who proposed that all snorers put on their gas masks before sleeping. It wasn't the most comfortable way to catch some shut-eye, but it worked.

Another problem was the noise of rain hitting our ponchos. It made a very different sound than rain falling on vegetation, and could be identified by the enemy. We hit on the idea of using captured Vietcong ponchos. They were made with very soft plastic, so they didn't make noise in the rain. We took to wearing them on our night patrols.

Ironic that the best equipped army in the world discarded its rain gear and used the enemy's.

35. Check Six

"Check six" is a well-known pilot's warning. Six o'clock is your rear. Always check your six to see whether you are being trailed. In my second war, I had to administer mouth-to-mouth to a dying paratrooper, who was one of four casualties from an ambush. We had been trailing an enemy patrol for more than an hour, when we were attacked from the rear. The enemy patrol had simply doubled back—trailed us—and then attacked. In my third war, even with all our previous experience, we fell into three ambushes.

To prevent ambushes, we instituted what we called the zigzag requirement. Our rule was that we would not march longer than one hour in a straight line. After one hour, we had to change our direction of march. Also, if we were in areas where we thought there might be enemy soldiers, we would stop and stay as quiet as possible for two minutes or more, so we could hear everything that was happening around us. We would frequently double back to see if anybody was following us, and on one occasion, captured three Viet Cong soldiers who were trailing us.

Checking where you have been may be as important as checking where you are going.

36. One Hundred Men for One Tank

Tanks played a significant role in Vietnam. Before this third combat tour, I had been convinced that armor could not be used effectively in thick jungle, but I was wrong. By the end of the tour, I would have traded a company of soldiers for one armored vehicle.

In the jungle, most of our casualties were caused by booby traps or by enemy fire from field fortifications that we couldn't see until we were on top of them. We sustained many casualties because of this. A tank moving through the jungle does something a soldier cannot do— it crushes the vegetation in front of it and explodes booby traps that could have killed or injured a man. These same booby traps do almost nothing to a tank. As the vehicle pushes through trees and vegetation, the debris also covers the flank ports of the enemy's pill boxes. This forces the enemy soldier to come out of his hole and engage the tank with an antitank weapon. At that point, our infantry can protect the tank by engaging the enemy soldier in the open. Light armor has an important role in jungle fighting.

I learned not to dismiss any idea until I had at least tried it once.

37. Fear of the Unknown

On one occasion, we encountered poison gas. It had a devastating effect on our unit, demoralizing a company in a very short time. We had been out in the jungle for almost ten days, when we saw a Viet Cong sniper who had just fired run into a hole. We followed him, and a volunteer went inside the hole with ropes around him so that we could retrieve him. When we pulled him back to the surface, he collapsed. The medics who gave him mouth-to-mouth resuscitation also collapsed. Within five minutes, we had four casualties around the hole.

We moved these soldiers away from the area and placed a charge where we thought the cave was. When we exploded the charge, gas was released into the air from the hole. We yelled for everyone to mask. Four soldiers lost consciousness. Fear began to spread that the gas masks were not providing protection against this particular gas. As blisters began to appear on the soldiers' skin, someone yelled, "Mustard gas!" and we had panic on our hands. Our chemical experts were unable to tell us what type of gas we had encountered, but we were told that it had not been the much feared mustard gas.

―――――――――

Losing confidence in our equipment or leaders is the enemy's greatest weapon.

38. Chaplains in Combat

Our chaplains were crucial to morale. I used them with our front line troops. Because of this, a senior chaplain criticized me for exposing our chaplain too often to combat. My answer was: He is where the men need him, where there are wounded and dying. When he's back in the chapel, in the rear, none of the soldiers who really need him can get to him. I went so far as to close the chapel to encourage the chaplain to spend most of his time with troops in difficult areas. One of our chaplains in the Brigade was awarded the Medal of Honor, the highest valor award in the military.

———————————————

"Valor is a gift. Those having it never know for sure whether they have it until the test comes. And those having it in one test never know for sure if they will have it when the next test comes." (Carl Sandburg)

39. Is Congress a Pain?

Congressional representatives were interested in what we were doing in Vietnam. Many soldiers corresponded with their legislators, usually to complain about something. The rule in our unit was that we had to answer congressional mail within 24 hours after it was received, even when we were in combat. The usual query concerned such things as why wasn't a particular soldier getting a shower, or getting his mail on time. Congressional interest was welcomed. It gave us an opportunity to contact our legislators and explain our needs.

Dear Representative (Name):

We very much appreciate the interest you have taken in our soldiers fighting for the security of the United States in Vietnam. We don't resupply our soldiers daily out in the field, for fear that the helicopters will give away their positions. The same holds true for providing troops with showers when they are out on patrol for five or more days. Rest assured that the commanders of our soldiers have their best interests at heart. Thank you for your concern.

Respectfully yours,

"Remember your leaders...consider the outcome of their way of life and imitate their faith." (Hebrews 13:7)

Enemy Fire Kills U.S. General, The Fifth to Die in Vietnam War

By The Associated Press

SAIGON, South Vietnam, April 1—Brig. Gen. William R. Bond, commander of the United States 199th Light Infantry Brigade, was killed by enemy small-arms fire today. He was the fifth American general killed in action in the Vietnam war—the four others died in aircraft crashes.

General Bond, who was 51 years old and from Portland, Me., was struck in the chest by a bullet about 70 miles northeast of Saigon. He died within minutes after reaching an Army field hospital.

Military spokesmen said his command and control helicopter had landed in the area along the southeastern edge of War Zone D. He was shot after he got out to inspect a patrol that had been in contact with Vietcong troops during stepped-up enemy activity.

"Apparently he had gotten out of the helicopter and was walking when he was hit," said a spokesman. "He was not very far away from the helicopter.

His pilot flew him to the hospital."

The spokesman said it was possible that General Bond had been hit by a sniper's bullet. Contact earlier in the day indicated enemy troops remained in the region.

General Bond took command of the 199th Brigade Nov. 28, replacing Maj. Gen. Warren K. Bennett. He had served one previous tour in Vietnam and had also served in Thailand.

He had more than 26 years active duty in the Army. He was deputy director of the international and civil affairs directorate of the Department of the Army before returning to Vietnam last year. He was promoted to brigadier general in August, 1969.

General Bond held the Silver Star, the Legion of Merit with Oak Leaf clusters, the Bronze Star with Oak Leaf and the Purple Heart.

He held a bachelor's degree from the University of Maryland.

A graduate of the Army War College and other senior service schools, General Bond held a number of key staff posts at Army headquarters during his career.

He first was in Vietnam in 1959-1960, when the United States had a small advisory mission there.

General Bond's wife was reported to be on a trip to Colombia.

The last American general killed in Vietnam was Maj. Gen. Keith Ware, commanding general of the Army's First Infantry Division, who died in a helicopter crash in 1968. Maj. Gen. Bruno A. Hochmuth, commander of the Third Marine Division, also was killed in a helicopter crash.

Maj. Gen. Robert F. Worley, vice commander of the Seventh Air Force, was killed when his RF-4 Phantom jet was shot down, and Maj. Gen. William J. Crumm, commander of the Third air Division, died when two B-52 bombers collided en route to a mission in Vietnam.

Associated Press
Brig. Gen. William R. Bond

40. A General is Killed

Our Brigade Commander, General Bond, took many chances. He was constantly with our troops in combat. One day, an enemy sniper shot him through the chest. He died in the evacuation helicopter. It has been said that in the modern battlefield, death beats one tune for the soldier and another for the General in the rear. General Bond was not a typical General.

General Bond was a soldier's General. He was a humble, brave and caring man. He was killed demonstrating that Generals need to share the risks they ask their men to take.

If more world leaders did the fighting, we would surely have fewer wars.

41. A Letter to a Mother

Years after my Vietnam experience, I read a letter that a Marine Colonel had written to the mother of one of his dead marines in World War II. Here is part of it:

> "*We who survive must work for the objectives for which your son died: that tolerance, understanding and harmony may be established in human relationships. Only through an honest regard on the part of each individual for the welfare of others can we hope to obliterate the tragedy of war. Only then will your sacrifice have a measure of justification. It is not given to us to know the process by which certain of us are chosen for sacrifice while others remain. As I ponder the names of those who are selected for the sacrifice, it seems to me as if the most worthy among us are the ones who died.*"

I wish I had seen this before writing my own 34 letters to parents of young men who would never return home.

We will never be able to do enough to console parents for the loss of their sons.

Part Three:

SERVING IN PEACETIME

42. The American Tree Officer

During the 1960s, two years of duty in Brazil offered a welcome rest before going once again to war. I arrived at a time of turmoil. The Brazilian military was about to oust a civilian-led government and begin a long stay in power. As a reminder of these times, I kept copies of censored newspapers with most of their front pages left blank because they didn't meet with the censor's approval. As I traveled, I was surprised at the size of Brazil and its jungles. It is larger than the continental United States, with a population greater than that of all the South American republics combined.

My most memorable event was leading a parachute jump in the middle of the Amazon jungle. Because of a strong desire to avoid falling into a river full of alligators and man-eating fish, I opted for jumping into the trees. After that jump, I was affectionately called the American Tree Officer. I left this assignment with a healthy respect for dense jungle, the need for light, long-range communications, and skilled navigators. Being lost in the Amazon is perilous.

I also saw the effects of a relatively sedentary life compared to that of a jungle hunter. Two tribes that lived within 15 miles of each other showed marked differences in their physical development. The people who ate meat and spent much of their time tracking and hunting animals for food were strong, tall and healthy. Those who were farmers were smaller, and appeared to be less healthy and strong.

When in doubt, choose trees.

The President and Mrs. Clinton
request the pleasure of your company
at a reception to be held at

The White House
on Thursday, May 4, 1995
at four o'clock

In celebration of the

Thirtieth Anniversary of the
White House Fellowships
Program

43. The White House

A month before the end of my third combat tour, one of our clerks handed me an application for the White House Fellows. This Fellowship was established in 1964 by John Gardner, who was then Secretary of Health, Education and Welfare under Lyndon Johnson. The program identifies young leaders, brings them to the White House for a year, and then returns them to their professions. I spent my one-year White House Fellowship as a Staff Officer in the national Security Council.

Secretary Gardner used to remind us that when this nation was only two million strong, we had Washington, Jefferson, Lincoln, Hamilton and other exceptionally great men to lead us. He would then ask, "Now that we are over 200 million strong, where are the Washingtons and the Jeffersons?" The White House Fellows Program gives promising young leaders a taste of top-level service, in hopes of making them better leaders when they return to their communities.

The competition is stiff. From the 2,000 or more who apply, only 15-18 are chosen. Candidates go though a series of interviews, fill out many long forms, write essays, and have to submit to extensive background checks. The culmination of the competition is an assignment in the White House or with one of the Cabinet Officers. Many White House Fellows have risen to positions of prominence. Alumni have been senators, governors, college presidents, admirals and generals. One White House Fellow became the highest ranking officer in the U.S. military.

I always kid General Colin Powell that I made him famous. He was a Fellow as a young Colonel. I was then Director of the Fellows Program and assigned him to "Cap" Weinberger, who was then head of the Office of Management and Budget. Weinberger later became Secretary of Defense and brought Powell along to work for him. Colin Powell is such an outstanding leader and human being that his star would have risen even if he had never been a Fellow.

Expose the young to outstanding education and most will become outstanding.

44. Working for Kissinger

May 10, 1971

Dear Foy:

I am writing to you to recommend Lt. Colonel Bernard Loeffke
for admission to your graduate program for completion of his
Ph. D. in international relations. Col. Loeffke is a White House
Fellow and has served this year on the National Security Council
staff, where I have had a chance to observe his abilities. I
recommend him to you most highly.

He would like to specialize in Soviet-Latin American relations,
and I believe him particularly well qualified for advanced work
in this field. He has a masters degree in the Russian language
and Soviet area studies. He is fluent in Russian, Spanish,
Portuguese and French. He has taught Russian and served as an
interpreter. At the NSC, Col. Loeffke has done high-quality
analytical work in many different fields and has made an important
contribution to the preparation of policy papers for me and for the
President. His background in international affairs is considerable.
He has served three tours in Southeast Asia while in the U.S.
Army, and has also spent time in Brazil. His record of service in
the Army is exceptional.

I believe he would be an asset to your program, and I hope you
can give his application favorable consideration.

Warm regards,

Henry A. Kissinger

Professor Foy D. Kohler

In 1970, The National Security Council (NSC) was headed by Dr.
Henry Kissinger, who used to say that those who worked for him had to
demonstrate three qualities. First was loyalty. Once you accepted the
job, all your previous loyalties must disappear. The second quality was
stamina. He felt that it wasn't useful to be brilliant if you couldn't work
long hours on a daily basis. He expected his people to work seven days
a week, 15 to 16 hours a day. The third quality was competence, which,
at least at this level of government, was generally easy to find.

The NSC acts as a funnel of information for the President, and is run by the Assistant to the President for National Security Affairs. Its staff varies according to the advisor. During the 1970s, most NSC staff came from the State Department, with some from the intelligence agencies and a few from the military. The NSC presents to the President, in option form, the views of various departments. For example, if we were to formulate a strategy for Latin America, we would need opinions and information from Treasury, State, CIA, the Military, Agriculture, Commerce, and so on. All these positions need to be put into a format that can be presented to the President.

I worked in an office that reviewed many of the papers prepared for Dr. Kissinger. There were four of us: John Glancy, a lawyer, who had served as clerk for a Supreme Court Justice; Chet Crocker, a university professor; John Negroponte, an officer from the State Department; and me, representing the Military. Glancy would review a paper to see if it was binding and written in accordance with the law. Crocker checked to see that we were considering historical lessons learned. Negroponte saw that these documents reflected the agreements with other governments and dovetailed with foreign policy strategy. I provided a military view. The more we discussed a recommendation, the clearer the advantages and disadvantages became.

Dr. Kissinger had us write objectives for every region of the world. He then published those goals in an unclassified booklet, which detailed what the United States foreign policy would be. It was time consuming, but it forced us to formulate a clear vision. Once that vision and our strategy were written down, our work became easier.

"Without a vision, the people perish." (Proverbs)

45. Formulating a Strategy

There were similarities between some of the things that we did in the Army and what we did in the White House. I had been taught that a strategy has three components: what is to be done, how it is to be done, and who is going to do it

In the White House, Dr. Kissinger used to demand that at least three but no more than five options be presented. He would often become annoyed if we presented less-than-satisfactory options. The first of the three he would label as idiocy, the second as lunacy, and the third as obvious. He would complain that we were not serving the President well by presenting such options. He also demanded that every option considered the cost of taking that action. In other words, every option had to have a dollar sign attached to it. This experience taught me that a presentation has to be concise, with facts and cost considerations.

The problem with a strategy in a democratic society is that it may change with a change in administration. In a democracy, when the President changes, most of the White House staff also changes. This happens in domestic as well as foreign policy. New players need time to get their feet on the ground and to articulate strategies. It is also difficult to get a team effort from such different backgrounds. To form a cohesive team out of this group requires leaders with vision, enthusiasm, and positive personal qualities.

To create a strategy, answer the What, How and Who.

Dr. Henry A. Kissinger, Assistant to the President for National
Security Affairs

Brig. Gen. Alexander M. Haig, Deputy Assistant to the President
for National Security Affairs

WHITE HOUSE SITUATION ROOM - David Y. McManis - V. James Fazio

NSC STAFF
OFFICE OF THE ASSISTANT FOR NATIONAL SECURITY AFFAIRS
Robert Houdek
Peter Rodman
LCdr Jonathan Howe, USN
David Young
Winston Lord

NSC STAFF SECRETARIAT
Jeanne W. Davis
D. Keith Guthrie
John Murphy
Harry Beach

OPERATIONS STAFF

LATIN AMERICA
Viron P. Vaky
Arnold Nachmanoff
Mary Brownell

EAST ASIA
John Holdridge
Richard Smyser
Herbert Levin

UN AFFAIRS & LONG RANGE PLANNING
Marshall Wright
John Lehman

PLANNING AND COORDINATION
GROUP
Col. Richard Kennedy, USA
Chester Crocker
John Glancy
Lt. Col. Bernard Loeffke, USA
John Negroponte

EUROPE
Helmut Sonnenfeldt
William Hyland
Arthur Downey

PROGRAM ANALYSIS STAFF
Wayne Smith
John C. Court
Robert J. Ryan, Jr.
Capt. Robert L. Sansom, USAF
John A. Hamilton
Dennis N. Sachs

NEAR EAST AND SOUTH ASIA
Harold Saunders
Samuel Hoskinson
Rosemary Neaher

AFRICA
Marshall Wright
Fernando Rondon
INTERNATIONAL ECONOMIC
AFFAIRS
C. Fred Bergsten
Ernest B. Johnston
Robert Hormats

SCIENTIFIC AFFAIRS
Col. Robert M. Behr, USAF
Michael A. Guhin

94

46. It Was Exhausting

In the White House, we literally worked seven days a week, 15-plus hours a day. We often slept on our sofas, showered and ate in our offices. Dr. Kissinger worked us hard, and we were often exhausted. Dr. Kissinger's military assistant at the time was General Alexander Haig. General Haig understood leadership. He would give Dr. Kissinger the names of our spouses. Kissinger would then call and tell them how important our work was. Human beings need to be stroked, and the phone calls provided some of these strokes.

I learned that the White House is staffed by the same human beings that are found in other areas of the bureaucracy. Most of our time in the National Security Council (NSC) was spent trying to contain crises. At times I felt frustrated because I knew that I had done better work in the Army Staff. Because of the crisis atmosphere, we often didn't have time to consult or to rewrite drafts.

What exhausted us most were mental stress and fatigue. In the Army, at least we were physically as well as mentally pushed, and our health was generally good. For many civilians, that important physical outlet is missing. In my one year at the NSC, I saw many burned out individuals, with one person being carried out on a stretcher.

"If anything is excellent or praiseworthy, think about such things." (St. Paul, Philippians 4:8)

What separates a mediocre from an outstanding leader? Those who put their free time to good use will be outstanding. We don't have to be geniuses, but we definitely need to study the problems that we are attempting to solve. Solutions don't often come with eight-hour days. If our leisure time is put to good use by learning speed reading, writing, and other skills that are relevant to our professions, we will be outstanding. I would also add the need to be concise. Make presentations short and enthusiastic. Learn to write well. Busy officials have no time for long-winded subordinates and those who rely on countless training aids. The ability to write clearly is critical. I have known many officials who, when asked what they want most of their subordinates, have answered "the ability to write well."

Speed reading and speed writing were invaluable. Speed reading allowed me to digest many pages and meet deadlines. Speed writing helped in taking thorough notes. I also came to appreciate the importance of understanding foreign languages. On more than one occasion, I have seen an interpreter misconstrue what was being said, and the official never knew that it had happened. Interpreters must be checked, and having an assistant verify what is said is crucial.

I learned that foreign policy can be influenced by private citizens, who can produce well thought out, well researched, well presented short papers. The NSC received many unsolicited papers on different subjects. Often, they were useful. Dr. Kissinger also asked "think tanks" to come up with analyses, as they had time to ponder alternatives, while we did not. We were always under the pressure of extinguishing the burning issues of the day. Pressure groups are very effective when they provide well-written, thoughtful papers to congressional or White House staffers, who never have enough time.

"I will prepare myself, and my chance will come." (Abraham Lincoln)

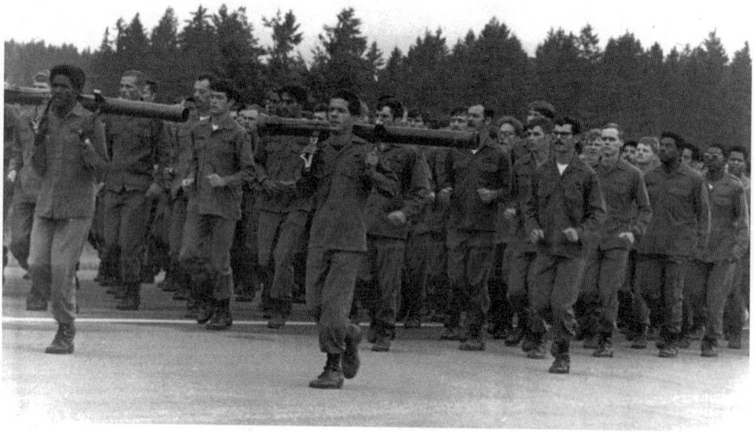

48. Motivating in Peacetime

Many of us felt that leading men in peacetime was harder than leading them in combat. In war, boredom is replaced by fear, and training is accepted as a way to help stay alive.

Commanding more than 3,000 infantrymen in a peacetime atmosphere challenged me. Most of my previous commands had been with Vietnam as an objective. Now, in the middle 1970s, Vietnam was history.

I thought I was demanding, but fair. Others thought I was too demanding. Our officers had to do everything their troops had to do, plus a little more. The officers ran with 20-pound radios on their backs, while most of their troops ran without added weights, except for volunteers, who carried recoilless rifles. Another requirement was wrestling in the "Bear Pit." All officers had to jump in and wrestle their men.

This and my other activities drew criticism from some officers who stuck to more conservative and traditional ways. However, my Commanding General, Volney Warner, loved it.

I have been influenced by some of history's greatest combat leaders: Wallace in Ireland, Hannibal in Europe, Rommel in Germany, San Martin in South America, Patton in the U.S. All of these leaders led from the front, giving credence to the infantry's call in combat of, "Follow me!" These great leaders also cared and their soldiers knew it.

Leadership is the art of influencing others to enthusiastically accomplish our goals.

49. THE BEAR PIT

Problem = Frustration. Solution = The Bear Pit. The pit is composed of a 24' in diameter sand-covered area with a 3' high sandbag wall. Officers and soldiers stand opposite. When the call is given, the two groups rush each other. Sweat-soaked bodies slam together, as the two teams try to win by throwing all members of the opposition over the wall.

When a soldier is allowed to wrestle with an officer, he gains more respect for that leader. In turn, the officer ends up with more respect for the soldier. Although many people wrestle in the pit at one time, it is not a helter-skelter contest without rules. No neck or head holds are allowed. A two-minute time limit is allotted for the teams to dump as many members of the other team as possible over the wall.

The pit is great for morale and it builds stamina. The first mark of a good soldier is stamina. Our daily runs with recoilless rifles, mortars, radios and individual weapons, plus the frequent fights in the Bear Pits, trained us to perform, even when we were on the brink of exhaustion.

Experiences that make you look fear in the face teach you courage and confidence. They also enable you to say, "I lived through this...I can take the next thing that comes along."
(Eleanor Roosevelt)

50. TRAINING IN ALASKA

It's a tough challenge to lead men and women in Alaska at 40 degrees below zero. When I took over the command of our 3,000-member brigade, I had less than three months to get us ready for winter maneuvers in the "Land of the Bear." I had to prove to our soldiers that they were tough and able to sustain hardships in conditions of extreme cold.

We instituted goals that appeared beyond reach. We began with a selected group of 30 soldiers from each of the three main units of the Brigade. These 90 men ran 20 miles in boots. Each group of 30 men carried a machine gun and a recoilless rifle, and every soldier carried a gas mask and rifle.

At the end of the 20 miles, there was a tactical exercise. During this exercise, they established radio communications with a rear area, placed demolition charges on an obstacle, and simulated directing fire from attack helicopters. They also interrogated a prisoner, fired live rounds at a mock machine-gun nest, and simulated destruction of enemy-held buildings through the use of practice hand grenades. They then ran an additional mile to a helicopter pick-up site.

The example of these 90 men showed the rest of the brigade that what seemed impossible was within reach. This reminded me of the old song, "Give me some men who are stout hearted men, who will fight for the right they adore. Start me with ten who are stout hearted men, and I'll soon give you ten thousand more!"

51. Troubles in Panama

During 1987-89, Panama experienced more repression than I had seen in any communist country. The real troubles began after General Manuel Noriega stole the 1988 presidential election. People were peacefully protesting and getting beaten up. Noriega's "Dobermans," his security thugs, were out in the streets 24 hours a day. I spent a year and a half watching Panamanians being brutalized by Noriega's Popular Defense Forces.

U.S. Military Headquarters was not in downtown Panama City, but we had 1,200 U.S. military families living downtown. During the riots, my wife and I made it a point to visit the riot areas at least three evenings a week. There was no electricity, no water in many of the apartments. Our visit was to reassure the military families, but when Noriega's forces became confrontational, we had to withdraw those families from their homes. While I was commanding general in Panama, leading up to Operation Just Cause, we had 59 fire fights with Noriega's people. Marc, our son, was born during one of these fire fights.

We protected our soldiers by using deception. I learned the value of deception during my three years as Defense Attaché in China. I thought I knew something about war, until I went to China and saw their deception techniques. I had already been in combat for four years during three tours of Vietnam, and I had been Army Attaché in the Soviet Union, but I was still on a steep learning curve. In China, I learned that a general first looks for ways his troops might deceive the enemy. Then, he looks at camouflage. With this in mind, we designed our defensive setup in Panama.

Noriega's forces would probe our defenses by firing at American checkpoints on roads. Their objective was to provoke us into firing back into civilian traffic, thereby creating a popular reaction against the American presence. As a result, we had to create restrictive rules of engagement. It took self-control not to respond.

"In war, truth is so precious that it must be guarded by a thousand lies." (Winston Churchill)

52. Who Goes There?

We never had enough people, so I had to place maintenance soldiers on guard duty. One young woman asked me, "General, how many times do I have to yell 'Halt!' before I do something?" That was a good question, because Noriega's Forces knew our rules were that we didn't put a bullet into a rifle chamber unless we felt that bodily harm was about to be committed to our people. The procedure was to yell "Halt!" in Spanish. If the suspicious person continued forward, and you could identify that they were armed, then you could chamber the round. Next, you yelled, "Halt, or I will fire!"

We knew that members of Noriega's "Dignity Battalions" were trained to infiltrate American bases, so we ordered deception to be integrated into our defensive tactics. Before our soldiers went out on guard duty, each one had to build a life-size mannequin. I ordered that the dummies be made fully visible, in case there was a sniper attack. We put our people ten feet away from the dummy guard. Every 45 minutes, we moved the figure to create a lifelike illusion. We had two dummies that were fired on. They saved the lives of the real guards.

One night, I was the biggest "dummy." I spoke to one of these decoys for at least 45 seconds. A signal unit had placed a dummy with a helmet and a rubber M-16 rifle. They rigged it like a puppet, with an audio voice recorder. When I approached, the dummy came out of the dark. I heard, "Halt!" The "guard" pulled his weapon forward. When I heard "Who goes there?" I identified myself. Then I heard, "Advance and be recognized!" I was embarrassed and proud to find that the real guard was a signal sergeant who was pulling a cord in the shadows. He received the ingenuity award we gave each night to soldiers who built the most realistic decoy.

Give your people a challenge, and they will often pleasantly surprise you.

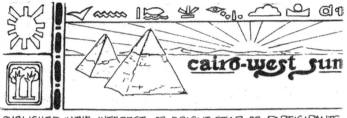

cairo-west sun

PUBLISHED IN THE INTEREST OF BRIGHT STAR 85 PARTICIPANTS

July 31, 1985   Number 2

Corps is ready to go

By Capt. Richard L. Ellwood

"Our mission is to deploy anywhere in the world, and upon arrival be prepared to fight--and win," said Brig. Gen. Bernard Loeffke, XVIII Airborne Corps chief-of-staff.

"We are always on the move, going somewhere every month. We have recently trained in Alaska, Panama, and California," Loeffke added.

The corps is participating in the Bright Star 85 exercise with elements of the 101st Airborne Div., 24th Infantry Div., and support units.

The 82nd Airborne Div. soon will be conducting a personnel and equipment air drop as their introduction to Bright Star.

Loeffke explained that the 18th must be prepared to depart for any notice, so preparedness is a key factor in deployment. The corps recently accomplished this mission by moving a large part of the command from its headquarters at Ft. Bragg, N.C. to San Francisco using a combination of air, sea and road transportation.

The 18th is the Army's "contingency corps," said Loeffke, because of its ability to be used anywhere. Asked to compare Bright Star 85 with other exercises, the general emphasized that, "By our participating in Bright Star, we are reaffirming the corps' mission as the 'cutting edge.' We can go any place, any time."

Bright Star poses many special obstacles to the 18th, especially in navigation and identifying terrain.

Lt. Col Michael Loesekann of the corps G-3 explained that military personnel "are faced with vast differences in distance and terrain features. They have to use aerial photos to supplement their maps.

"And our aviators must often fly at dusk, nighttime, or at first light because of the high winds during the day."

The corps will be conducting at least two major jumps during Bright Star. One of the jumps will involve joint training with Egyptian airborne troops.

TO THAT, BRIG. GEN. LOEFFKE SAID,

"LET THOSE WHO WISH US ILL TRY US."

The second operation will be a strategic jump in which elements of the 82nd Airborne Div. will fly directly from Ft. Bragg to Egypt, refueling en route, and drop personnel and heavy equipment.

Those troops will then link up with Marine Corps amphibious forces. These combined units will then conduct an intra-theater airlift to Cairo West.

Both Loeffke and Loesekann are positive about U.S. Forces training in Egypt. "Egypt is a proven participant in exercises like this," said Loeffke. "And Bright Star is building our methods and techniques for merging Egyptian and U.S. forces for training," said Loesekann, adding "the airborne's participation in Bright Star is crucial and the armor with air cavalry mix is right."

What do the troops think of Bright Star? Pfc. Tracy Conboy had this to say about the desert environment: "I'm from Arizona," she said, laughing, "I love it."

On being an airborne soldier, Specialist Johnny Hood had this story: "My father was retired Special Forces--it seemed like a real challenge--and I felt obliged to do the same."

But with all of the world-wide challenges facing the XVIII Airborne Corps, can this highly mobile unit effectively respond?

To that, Loeffke said, "Let those who wish us ill try us."

53. Paratroopers are Ready to Go

I have been lucky to have been led by some of the greatest military commanders in the world. Among them were Generals Hank Emerson, Volney Warner and Jim Lindsay.

Two tours of combat with the same commander served to forge a strong bond. General Lindsay had been a paratrooper advisor with the Vietnamese in 1964, at the same time I had. Five years later, he became a Battalion Commander, and asked me to be his deputy again in combat. I learned how to lead large units in battle from this incredible soldier. His coolness under fire, knowledge of tactics and love for his troops were good examples to emulate. I used what I learned from him when I was given a similar unit to command in combat. Our friendship continued, and when he became the Commander of the Army's Parachute Corps, he asked me to be his Chief of Staff. General Lindsay is godfather to my son, Marc.

The Parachute Corps had more than 40,000 troops and was the Army's contingency unit. This meant that whenever there was a problem anywhere in the world, we were the first to go. To be ready to operate anywhere, we had to train everywhere.

We rehearsed with frequent deployments to the Middle East. Troops would board airplanes in North Carolina, refuel in the air over Morocco, and then, after almost a day and night in the air, jump into Egypt near the pyramids. Often, our tanks and heavy equipment followed on Navy ships. It was a strong message of our capabilities to both friend or foe. Years later, it would serve us well in Operation Desert Storm.

"Repetition is the mother of learning." (Russian proverb)

CONGRATULATIONS

George Bush

FOR SPONSORING KILOMETER 1 AND CONTRIBUTING
TO THE 1492 KILOMETER ANNIVERSARY FRIENDSHIP RUN

MG Bernard Loeffke, U.S. Army (Ret.)
Co-Chairman, Childrens' Fund

João Baena Soares
Secretary General, Organization of American States

54. The Long Run

My next-to-last military assignment was as Chairman of the Inter American Defense Board. This organization is composed of the senior military officers of the Americas and the Caribbean. One of the Board's missions is to improve relations between the militaries of the hemisphere. Another is to strengthen civil-military relations, which in some countries have been traditionally weak.

We were constantly looking for ways to become better acquainted, and the 500th anniversary of the discovery of the Americas gave us that opportunity. We came up with the idea of a 500-kilometer run that would include military and civilian runners from every nation. We chose to run 250 kilometers in Argentina and 250 kilometers in Chile. The Argentinean portion of the run was selected to eulogize one of the greatest soldiers who ever lived. General San Martin accomplished the incredible feat of leading his troops over the Andes (14,000 feet high) to defeat the Spanish armies in Chile.

It took us 14 days to run the 250 kilometers that General San Martin traveled centuries before. We started at the City of Mendoza with almost 1,000 runners, and ended with 35 runners at 14,000 feet. I pushed Marc, my son, a mile a day in a running stroller, while his mother drove in the support vehicle. Sharing a tough run made us all better friends.

"Let us run with perseverance the road marked out for us. Let us throw off everything that hinders." (Hebrews 12:1)

111

Part Four:

THE OLD RUSSIA

55. What Happened?

The Russia of today is very different from the Russia of the 1970s. Russia has come a long way. The transformation has been the result of many pressures. Religion is one of them.

I don't remember many lectures at West Point. The only one that stuck is the talk that Bishop Fulton Sheen gave. He ended his remarks on the Soviet Union by saying, "A nation that does not believe in God cannot last 50 years." The year was 1956. He has been proved right.

The Russia of the '70s was one of secrecy, lies and oppression. In the 1990s, Russia became more open and discussions are now more useful. This once great empire continues to be dangerous. It is the only country that still has the capability to destroy the U.S. in 20 minutes or less. Fear and curiosity make us want to know more. When I returned after three years in the old Russia, I tried to answer some of the many questions asked of me. To this day, I don't have many answers.

"A state that ignores the will and the rights of its citizens can offer no guarantee that it will respect the will and the rights of other peoples, nations, and states. A lasting peace and disarmament can only be the work of free people." (Havel)

56. Fish, Everywhere

In the 1970s, the Soviet officer was a graduate of one of 100-plus military academies. These institutions differed from West Point in that they focused on military subjects; West Point concentrated on a liberal education. The Soviet Union was not interested in providing a university education to its officers. It wanted to train them to be effective combat leaders, and many were needed. The following "fish story" explains why the Soviets felt they needed large armed forces.

During a conversation with a Soviet colonel, the colonel exclaimed that, as an American, I was fortunate. I responded, "Yes, I am proud to be an American." He replied, "I am not talking about pride. What I meant is that you are fortunate in your geographical location." When I asked him to explain, he asked, "What lies to the east of the United States?" I answered, "The Atlantic Ocean." He responded, "Yes, Atlantic fish." He then asked, "What lies to the west?" I said, "The Pacific Ocean." He answered, "Yes, Pacific fish." He then went on to ask what was to the north and to the south. I told him Canada and Mexico. He said, "Two nations that are smaller and weaker compared to yours. Americans are fortunate, for they have fish for neighbors to the east and west, and they have weak and friendly nations to the north and south. However, we in the Soviet Union have unstable borders on all sides, therefore, we need to have strong, large armed forces."

"There is neither East nor West, border, nor breed, nor birth, when two strong men stand face to face, though they come from the ends of the earth." (Rudyard Kipling)

115

57. One Nation, Many Nationalities

I had just started studying Russian, when I was invited to the Soviet embassy for a reception. While at the embassy, I had an opportunity to speak with one of the Soviet officials. I mentioned to him that he was the first Russian I had ever met. He interrupted and told me that he was a Soviet citizen, but not a Russian. He then explained that there were great differences between a Russian and a Georgian. This small exchange highlighted the vast differences that existed in the USSR. There were more than 100 nationalities, with different languages and different traditions.

One of these traditions was a game called "Catch the Girl." It was played in one of the central Asian republics. A woman on a horse starts the competition some ten meters in front of a man on a horse. When the whistle blows, the man has one minute to catch the woman and kiss her on the run. If he fails to catch and kiss her, then the positions are reversed with the man starting ten meters in front of the woman. When the whistle blows, she has one minute to try to catch the man and whip him as often as she can during that one minute.

This game was played monthly, but many Russians have never heard of it because they have never visited central Asia. Those who lived in the Russian republic knew little of what was going on in Azerbaijan, Uzbekistan or Moldavia. In the past, Soviets were restricted to Soviet republics and to their cities. They had internal passports, and they could not rent hotel rooms unless they had special passes from the government. In other words, they could not travel inside the U.S.S.R. without permission.

A Russian who became a close friend commented to me, "The car has made America the most mobile nation on earth." He then added, "It also helps that you don't need permission to travel from state to state."

117

СЕРТИФИКАТ

Настоящим удостоверяется, что символическая "МОНЕТА РАЗОРУЖЕНИЯ" изготовлена из металла советских ракет средней дальности Р—12, уничтоженных согласно советско-американскому Договору по РСМД.

Используемый металл не представляет опасности для Вашего здоровья.

"Монета" является уникальным сувениром и не может быть использована в качестве денежного знака.

CERTIFICATE

This is to certify that the token DISARMAMENT COIN is made of the metal of the R-12 (SS-4) Soviet medium range missiles scrapped under the Soviet-American INF Treaty.

The metal poses no harm for your health. The "coin" is a unique souvenir and cannot be used as currency.

58. We Have Met the Enemy

Exchange visits between Russian and U.S. cadets had been going on for many years. I went to West Point to participate in one of the early visits. I overheard several conversations, and the common thread was: "We have met the enemy, and they are like us!"

Russian Cadet

"I am impressed with the openness of Americans. My visit changed many of my perceptions. I thought Americans hated us, but I never saw an American who gave me a scowl. There was friendship in their faces. In New York, I was surprised at the tallness of the buildings."

West Point Cadet

"The Russian cadet was very much like I am. I had a stereotype of Russians. I felt comfortable with him, which is not what I thought I would feel. We need more of these exchanges. A good example is our history class. I felt that our teacher knew a lot, but he could not give us what the Russian cadet gave us—that is, personal perceptions. I liked him."

A Nuclear Missile Becomes a Peace Symbol

Soviet cadet Andrei Skubchenko, presented me with the Disarmament Coin. Andrei told me his father was a Soviet paratrooper who had asked him to present the only coin he had to a U.S. paratrooper. There was a certificate with the coin which read, "This is to certify that the Disarmament Coin is made out of the metal of the R-12 (SS4) Soviet Medium Range missiles destroyed under the Soviet American INF Treaty."

We are more alike than we are different.

59. First-Strike Mentality

A Soviet book called *First Strike* contains many statements by U.S. officials, such as ex-Secretary of Defense Schlesinger, whom it calls "mad dog" Schlesinger, because he created the doctrine of flexible nuclear response. This doctrine maintains that the U.S. would respond with tactical or strategic nuclear missiles, depending on the threat.

The book quotes General Patton as saying, during World War II, that the U.S. should keep going on to Moscow. It also quotes U.S. Air Force General LeMay, who stated that we should bomb the Soviet Union "back to the Stone Age." The conclusions of the author are that the United States has a first-strike capability in its missiles, and it has a first-strike mentality in its Generals. Capabilities of U.S. missiles and the mentality of its general officers equaled a first-strike strategy. Therefore, the Soviet Union preached that it needed to be well prepared for a nuclear attack.

This book was distributed down to the soldier level. In the 1990s, however, a new era dawned, and this type of book is no longer popular. We now cooperate more, disarm more and fear less. Our cooperation in the space program is one of many ways in which we are working together.

We don't see things as they are, we see them as we are.

60. Preparations for War

During the 1970s, the Soviet Union was not a country, but an army. Every school had a Soviet Officer who taught 140 hours of military instruction. During their last two summers in high school, children had to go to military sport camps, where they learned how to function in small combat units. Here they could earn the GTO badge (Gotof Trudu Oborone, which translates into Ready for Labor and Defense). Many requirements needed to be met in order to receive the GTO, including dummy hand grenade throwing, map reading, long distance running and swimming.

The GTO was administered to taxi drivers, to factory workers—in short, to all. I am reminded of my Soviet driver who told me he could not come to work on a Wednesday. When I asked him why, he said he was being tested for his GTO.

Prepare for war, and you may not have to fight one.

61. Nowhere to Hide

Russians have many fears. One of them is the fear of being invaded. Napoleon sacked Moscow in the 1800s, and Hitler's armies reached the outskirts of the city in the 1940s. This fear encouraged the construction of elaborate tunnels and civil defense training.

Civil defense training existed throughout the Soviet Union and was used to build morale. The training was widespread, with nuclear attack drills constantly being rehearsed. Movement by foreigners was restricted. We could move only within a two-and-one-half-mile radius from the center of Moscow, and could not leave the city without permission from Soviet authorities. Large portions of the Soviet Union were off limits. We reciprocated by restricting vast areas of the United States to them. Our suspicions of each other were intense. In truth, civil defense will matter little if there are massive nuclear exchanges. No matter what we do, no matter where we hide, we cannot ensure survival from a nuclear holocaust. This realization should be a strong motivator to keep talking until we reach a peaceful agreement.

―――――――――――――――

I cannot think of an instance in history when freely elected democracies fought each other.

62. THE BIGGER, THE BETTER

The Russians perceived themselves as surrounded by actual or potential enemies. A conversation with a Soviet general highlighted their apprehensive point of view: "We build our missiles big. You build yours small. Ours are big to scare would-be aggressors. They are useful both in peace and war. The size of our forces and weapons deter enemies. By contrast, you Americans build your missiles small but accurate. You can only use these missiles in war."

To the Soviet, the bigger, the better and the more, the safer.

"The future belongs to those who believe in the beauty of their dreams." (Eleanor Roosevelt)

November 6, 1970

MEMORANDUM FOR

HEADS OF ALL DEPARTMENTS AND AGENCIES
OF THE EXECUTIVE BRANCH

SUBJECT: Presidential Directive on Attendance at October
Revolution Anniversary Celebration at Soviet Embassy

In view of the continued unwarranted detention by Soviet authorities of
the crew and passengers of a light aircraft which inadvertently landed
on Soviet territory last month, including three officers of the US
Armed Forces, the President considers it inappropriate this year for
any Presidential appointee or any other member of the Executive Branch
of equivalent rank to attend parties at Soviet Embassies and Missions
observing the Anniversary of the October Revolution.

Heads of Departments and Agencies should ensure that attendance at
such parties by their subordinates be (a) limited in number and (b) con-
fined to officials of middle-level rank.

Heads of Departments and Agencies which do not normally have business
with the Soviet Government or its organizations should ensure that no
members of their Departments or Agencies attend such parties.

While it is not intended to volunteer a public statement explaining the
above measures, the following statement may be made in response to
questions:

"In view of the unwarranted detention of the crew and passengers of
a light American aircraft by Soviet authorities, including three
officers of the Armed Services of the United States, it is not deemed
appropriate this year for American officials to accept the hospitality
of the Soviet Government on the occasion of the November celebration.
This was a decision taken at the highest level."

The above actions will not be taken if the Soviets should release the crew
and passengers of the US aircraft before the parties in question occur.

Henry A. Kissinger

128

63. I'll Tell You Who Won

While I was traveling on a Soviet train from Murmansk to Moscow, I noticed a General come on board. He, his wife and I rode in the same car. After about an hour, I introduced myself and mentioned that our nations were growing closer together by working to limit strategic weapons. The General replied that he didn't think much would result from the meetings. He was very unfriendly.

I continued trying to make conversation, and pointed out that our leaders were at a summit with the express purpose of having friendlier relations. I mentioned that we had been allies during World War II in the common fight against Hitler. At this, he became quite animated, maintaining that the Soviet Union had done most of the fighting in World War II: "The United States came in at the end, when it was certain that Nazi Germany would be defeated." He emphasized that it was the Soviet Union that had won the war. It was the Soviet Union that had borne the majority of the casualties, and it was the Soviet Union that had defeated the bulk of the Nazi armies. He ended the conversation by saying, "Good day, colonel."

There was a Patton in the Soviet Union, and I had just met him. I am sure that there are other Pattons in the Russian army today. The ones we met in Moscow were politically oriented generals who did not easily reveal their feelings.

When there is hate, it is difficult to show politeness.

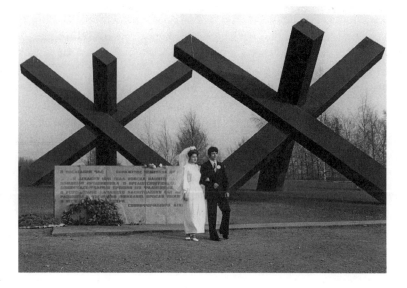

64. Patriotism...for What?

In the Soviet Union, I found strong patriotism that had been nurtured by reminders of the Nazi invasion. There were monuments everywhere to the atrocities committed by the Nazis. Soviet fear of being invaded appeared real. The memory of the incursion of the United States, Britain, France, and Japan after the end of World War I was taught to Soviet children.

Patriotism was carried to such an extent that many newly married couples paid respects to the war dead after the wedding. It was not uncommon to see a bride and groom go to a monument just within the limits of the city and honor the Soviets who died stopping the Nazi war machine eight miles from the center of Moscow.

The Russians have many fears. They fear the Chinese, and they fear turmoil within and outside of their borders. As far as the United States is concerned, they fear the Navy and the Air Force. Our Army is small compared to theirs, and was not widely feared until Desert Storm. Our Navy, on the other hand, is seen as a definite threat. U.S. submarines off the Norwegian coast cannot be detected. These submarines could have nuclear warheads on top of Russia within two or three minutes of launch. Russians fear the Air Force for its nuclear capabilities. They know that the United States has used nuclear weapons against Japan, and that, if need be, they would be used again.

Trust, but verify.

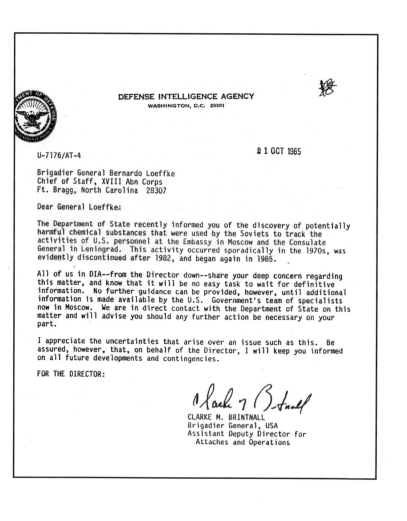

DEFENSE INTELLIGENCE AGENCY
WASHINGTON, D.C. 20301

U-7176/AT-4

2 1 OCT 1965

Brigadier General Bernardo Loeffke
Chief of Staff, XVIII Abn Corps
Ft. Bragg, North Carolina 28307

Dear General Loeffke:

The Department of State recently informed you of the discovery of potentially harmful chemical substances that were used by the Soviets to track the activities of U.S. personnel at the Embassy in Moscow and the Consulate General in Leningrad. This activity occurred sporadically in the 1970s, was evidently discontinued after 1982, and began again in 1985.

All of us in DIA--from the Director down--share your deep concern regarding this matter, and know that it will be no easy task to wait for definitive information. No further guidance can be provided, however, until additional information is made available by the U.S. Government's team of specialists now in Moscow. We are in direct contact with the Department of State on this matter and will advise you should any further action be necessary on your part.

I appreciate the uncertainties that arise over an issue such as this. Be assured, however, that, on behalf of the Director, I will keep you informed on all future developments and contingencies.

FOR THE DIRECTOR:

CLARKE M. BRINTNALL
Brigadier General, USA
Assistant Deputy Director for
Attaches and Operations

132

65. LIVING IN THE OLD RUSSIA

Those of us who served in the Soviet Union during the '70s lived in our apartments knowing that our conversations were monitored. Some couples had found listening devices inside their mattresses.

This was not paranoia. We were indeed at the mercy of the KGB (Soviet intelligence). If we tried to lose our unwanted escorts, the tires of our automobiles would be slashed or sand would appear in the carburetor of our cars. Some of us placed a penny on the top of the inside of the suitcase. Whenever the suitcase was opened, the penny would slide somewhere else in the suitcase. Another way to see if anyone had been in the apartment was to put a lump of sugar under the carpet. If the lump was crushed, someone had been there.

We were also exposed to many events detrimental to our health. Microwaves were beamed at us to pick up information that was either typed or spoken. The KGB would put powder on our doorknobs, so that they could use fingerprints to trace those with whom we had spoken. Our Russian maids would spray an invisible powder on the soles of our shoes so that, with the use of special goggles, we could be tracked at night. Some of this material was thought to be carcinogenic.

I was followed by security personnel everywhere I went. Even when I left parties in the middle of the night and chose to go running, I would have a security person trailing me in the park. They wanted to see if I was meeting someone or leaving a message for someone.

Living in Moscow was hazardous to health.

66. Détente

In the past, we had a nuclear-strategic relationship with the Soviets, while we have had an economic relationship with the Chinese. Our relationship with Russia has now taken on an economic flavor, although arms talks continue to be important. We need to strengthen the relationship, being careful that as we trust, we also verify. We should continue to strengthen détente.

I used to explain détente to soldiers with this illustration: Picture two archers who are facing each other with bowstrings that are taut. As they face each other, one takes a suspicious step, and one archer lets go of his arrow. The other one does the same. Both arrows strike the target, and both archers are killed. Under détente, the tension on the bowstrings of each of these archers is released slowly, until no tension remains. If a misunderstanding occurs, there is plenty of time for dialogue as both sides begin to pull back on their bowstrings.

"I sought my soul, but my soul I could not see. I sought my God, but my God eluded me. I sought my brother, and I found all three." (Unknown)

Soviet Soldiers Killed in Afganistan

67. What is Ours?

In 1979, during the height of the Sino-Vietnam War, I was riding on a Soviet train returning from the northern part of the Soviet Union, when I overheard a conversation between Soviet soldiers. One of them was saying, "We ought to go and fight those Chinese and teach them a lesson." Another responded, "But we don't want to do that, because there are too many of them, and we will never stop fighting."

There was great concern about a war with China. My tour in the Soviet Union convinced me that the greatest Soviet fear had always been the Chinese. They considered them irrational and they remembered that the Mongol invasion of the Soviet Union lasted for over 200 years. They blamed the Chinese, even though it really were the Mongols who invaded and conquered most of Russia. In the new Commonwealth, the Russian Republic continues to dispute borders with China. The fear will continue.

Hopefully, these two giants can make lasting peace. It benefits no one to have them at odds with each other.

─────────────────────────

"No man is an island." (John Donne)

Р А С С А Д К А

на заседании 22 ноября 1977 года

US SALT Seating Chart
US Mission
Tuesday, November 22, 1977
11:00 AM

Lt. Colonel Johnson	СМОЛИН В.В.
Colonel Loeffke	ЧУЛИЦКИЙ В.С.
Mr. Killham	КАРПОВ В.П.
Captain Pray	ЩУКИН А.Н.
Ambassador Earle	СЕЧЕНОВ В.С.
Mr. Rodzianko	БРАТЧИКОВ А.В.
Minister Perez	БЕЛЕЦКИЙ И.И.
Captain Kramer	ПАВЛИЧЕНКО В.П.
Dr. McNeill	БЕКЕТОВ Ю.Ф.
Mr. Nickels	

Interpreters:

БУЛАНЕНКО В.С.
СУДОНКИН Ю.В.

138

68. Sing It Off

In the '70s, during the Strategic Arms Limitation Talks in Geneva, a heated argument ensued between U.S. and Soviet delegations. Suddenly, General Rowny, the military representative, calmly took out his harmonica and started to play a tune!

The Soviets looked on with surprise. The faces that previously had been set into grimaces and scowls had now turned into chuckles and smiles. This unexpected bit of music had transformed the beast in us.

Music can calm the soul of even the toughest of Russian bears.

PART FIVE:

CHINA

69. THE MISSION

During the 1980s, the Army's Chief of Staff was General Meyer. As a young lieutenant in the 50s, he had deployed to Korea with an ill equipped and unprepared army. He recounted that, at one point, his unit was almost totally surrounded. He was in his foxhole when Chinese tanks approached his position. He stood up with his bazooka and fired a round at a tank no more than 15 meters away. To his dismay, the shell bounced off the armor. He had barely enough time to throw himself down in the foxhole and watch the Chinese tank roll over his position and shoot the infantrymen alongside of him.

As a result of that experience, Meyer decided that if he ever attained a senior leadership position, he would never send American soldiers with inferior equipment to fight a third-world country.

Meyer was also worried about the bad relations with the Chinese and wanted to change that situation. He called me in one day and gave me a simple mission: "I want you to go to China and make sure we never fight the Chinese again." When I asked if he had any more guidance, he said, "No. I leave the details up to you. Just make sure they become our friends and not our enemies."

This was how I became the first Army General to be Chief of the Military Mission in the People's Republic of China.

"If you would win a man to your cause, first convince him that you are his sincere friend." (Abraham Lincoln)

141

70. Stranger Equals Enemy

As part of his equipment during his journey through space, Senator John Glenn had been given a series of cards. These cards were to be used if he had to make an emergency landing. They were written in foreign languages, and Glenn was surprised to see that, in many languages, the words "stranger" and "enemy" were the same. The emergency landing never occurred, but other Americans have landed in the PRC and attempted to make a difference.

Stan Cottrell, the incredible U.S. athlete who ran 40 miles a day for 40 days, made a difference in Sino-U.S. relations with his great Friendship Run from the Great Wall of China to the tip of Southern China. At the time of the run, Cottrell was 50 years old. This hardy and ingenious American met more Chinese during his Friendship Run than any of us had in our years in China. Cottrell then invited three Chinese champion runners to the U.S. They ran from San Francisco to Washington, where they were greeted by President Bush.

In China, as anywhere, relationships are important. The concept of lao pengyo (old friend) is valued. There are many of us who are now considered old friends, but we need more friends.

"The glory of young men is their strength, and the beauty of old men is the gray head."
(Proverbs 20:29).

71. Wounded Generals

My first official function in China was to meet General Xu Xin. When I presented my credentials to the General, I mentioned that I had spent the better part of the night preparing for this meeting. I told him that, in one sense, he and I had little in common, as he had been the commander of Chinese forces in Korea against us when I was a young cadet at West Point.

However, I told him we did have something in common on the personal side. He had been wounded by U.S. artillery in Korea, and I had been wounded by Chinese mortars in Vietnam. I then added that my Chief of Staff had sent me to China to make sure we never exchanged ammunition that way again.

General Xu Xin stood up, shook my hand and said, "From the battlefields, we can become friends." Our relationship grew to be one of respect, and we then started to look for ways that our nations could become better friends. What we had in common included a desire for our nations to be strong, secure, and build a friendly working relationship that would benefit both countries.

"The art of being wise is the art of knowing what to overlook." (William James)

72. HALF A WIFE

Language and the difference in our cultures would continue to create misunderstandings between the Chinese and Americans. When General Xu Xin read my biography, he had a question about my qualifications. He had noticed that I was a midwife, which translates into Chinese as half a wife. The General was puzzled, and commented: "In China, you can only be a full wife or no wife at all, but very difficult to be a half a wife. Can you explain?" That was the first of many questions that we would try to answer for each other.

_____

When there is affection, the wrong word will be dismissed, for all will know it was not meant to offend.

73. THE BEAUTIFUL PEOPLE

Out of more than forty thousand ideograms in their language, the Chinese have chosen the ideogram "mei" to describe America. Mei means beautiful, and is derived from the ideogram for sheep. The Chinese consider sheep beautiful because the sheep provides milk, wool when sheared, and meat when slaughtered. When the Chinese want to say America, they have to say beautiful.

We are called the citizens of the beautiful country. America is beautiful. She is beautiful because she is good. She is beautiful because she is free. When America ceases being good, she will cease to be beautiful.

"Always do right. This will gratify some people and astonish the rest." (Mark Twain)

74. FEAR NOTHING

Effective ways to be accepted in a foreign land are by healing people, amusing them and identifying with them by having done something that they have done. I already knew a little medicine from my Special Forces training. Now I concentrated on singing, so that I could amuse my Chinese hosts.

I learned five Chinese songs well, and I sang them everywhere I went. I would introduce the songs with this statement: "Fear nothing on earth, fear nothing in heaven, only fear an American singing in Chinese." I would then proceed to destroy the song. The Chinese would laugh. Attempting to sing was all that was needed for me to be accepted.

"Laughter is the shortest distance between two people." (Victor Borge)

75. Health is Wealth

Before going to mainland China, I lived with a Chinese family in Hong Kong. I studied Chinese Mandarin ten hours a day. One of my instructors was an acupuncturist, and he would tell me the great interest that the Chinese have for health. He taught acupuncture and Chinese physical training. He introduced me to Mao's first book, which was on physical training. I also learned that the first commander of the Chinese Army, Zhu De, was a physical education instructor.

With my teacher's help, I wrote a small booklet on physical training in Chinese and English. I presented copies of this book to generals and Chinese officials, and found this an excellent vehicle to make friendships.

The first wealth is health. Without it, all other wealth matters little.

76. Lawyers Not Needed

"Why does a criminal need a lawyer if he is guilty? We do not try or accuse innocent people. Why would the police want to accuse an innocent person? In Western countries, lawyers defend guilty criminals, who, many times, go free. We don't allow this here," declared a Chinese official in 1974.

During the 1970s in the Peoples Republic of China, lawyers were considered unnecessary. The accused were hauled into courts composed of a judge and two lay persons, who had been elected by their neighbors. China felt that lawyers wasted the state's money and time defending guilty people.

The lack of defense counsels was still evident in 1982. In the summer of that year, I ran by one of the stadiums in Beijing. There were many trucks parked outside and a lot of noise was coming from inside the stadium. Within minutes, I saw people with cardboard signs draped around their necks being pushed into open trucks. On the cardboard was the name of the individual, with a big X scratched through the name. The X meant that this individual was dead. What it really meant was that the individual had been tried, sentenced, and was to be executed. In less than three hours, more than sixty Chinese had been tried, sentenced and executed. The condemned person was taken to an area where his neighbors, who were made to attend, could easily see the execution.

Death came quickly with a bullet fired into the head. The price of the bullet was charged to the individual's family.

"Forgive us the wrongs we have done, as we forgive the wrongs that others have done to us." (Matthew 6:12)

155

77. Humility and Honey Buckets

During the Chinese cultural revolution, the job of collecting human waste from the neighborhood latrines was reserved for the senior bureaucrats who had been demoted and disgraced. These individuals were seen coming down the streets at night pulling their carts full of excrement. Occupants of local households would come out and empty their honey buckets into the carts.

During the 1970s and early '80s, very few households had interior plumbing. In the capitol of the People's Republic of China, fewer than 40 percent of households had that luxury. The smell of "night soil" was evident in every town.

The cultural revolution caused great losses of capital, threw the nation into chaos, and created much human suffering. If there was one positive result, it was that it taught humility to the intellectuals of Chinese Society. It also exposed these deposed leaders to the harshness of Chinese life in the countryside.

"To serve the poorest of the poor, the sickest of the sick." (Mother Teresa)

78. ARE YOU AFRAID TO DIE?

I was traveling on a train in North Western China, when I heard a commotion at one of the stops. The conductor was saying, "Attention! We are traveling with foreigners, and there is an American General sitting on the right side of this car. Please make sure that you don't spit, and be sure to act with decorum." Soon, curious people started to come in.

A peasant approached me, asking, "Are you the American General?" When I replied that I was, he then questioned, "Are you afraid to die?" I wasn't sure where this conversation was going to lead, but I answered honestly, "Yes, I am afraid to die." The peasant volunteered, "Our generals are not afraid to die, and we have many troops in our army." He then asked if the United States had trains like the Chinese with restaurants in them. He obviously thought that China was a very modern nation.

This peasant continued by saying, "America should stop helping Taiwan. This is meddling in the affairs of China." The problem of Taiwan has long been a source of tension between the U.S. and the PRC. Throughout history, China has not considered itself united until Taiwan was part of the mainland. In 1991, Taiwan ceased to call the PRC the "Bandit Government." The PRC is now simply the communist government. Time heals wounds. Memories, hopefully, will fade. But for then, the peasant still wanted to know if American generals were as brave as Chinese generals.

"When I am afraid, O Lord almighty, I put my trust in you." (Psalms 56:3)

U.S. CASUALITIES IN 12 WARS

WAR	DATE	BATTLE DEATHS	OTHER DEATHS	TOTAL DEATHS	MIA	UNACCOUNTED FOR	NUMBERS SERVED
Revolutionary	1775-1783	6,824	18,500	25,324	8,445		
War of 1812	1812-1815	1,733	11,550	13,283	4,152		
Civil War	1861-1865	Union 140,414	224,097	364,511	281,881		
		Confederate 75,524	59,297	134,821	133,821		
Spanish America	1898	385	2,061	2,446	1,662		
World War I	1917-1918	53,513	63,195	116,708	204,002	3,350	4.7 Million
World War II	1941-1946	292,131	115,185	407,316	670,846	78,751	16 Million
Korea	1950-1953	33,629	20,617	54,246	103,284	8,200	5.7 Million
Vietnam	1964-1973	47,356	10,795	58,151	153,303	2,266	8.7 Million
Grenada	1983	18	0	18	116		
Panama	1989	21	0	21	200		.5 Million
Desert Storm	1991	146	0	146			

79. War is Inevitable

The Chinese had asked me to lecture on my experiences in the Soviet Union at the People's Liberation Army Academy. After I had concluded my remarks, I asked them to explain what they thought of Soviet-U.S. relations. The Chinese pulled out a huge map that was full of little light bulbs that could be turned on and off. They told me that the history of the Soviet Union started with a small circle, and the map showed Moscow within the circle. This circle slowly started to expand, showing how the Soviet Union, throughout the ages, had acquired more and more land from its neighbors. In the 1970s, it was two-and-one half times the size of the United States.

The Chinese said that the Soviet Union was a hungry country, and the word for Russia in Chinese sounds like the "hungry nation." They continued their lecture by showing many dots beginning to flash from inside the Soviet Union and traveling towards the U.S. There were also lights in the U.S. traveling towards the USSR. These lights represented nuclear exchanges between our two countries. The Chinese explained that war between the USA and the USSR was inevitable. When I asked what the Chinese would do during this war, they responded, "We will watch." The world has changed since then. Hopefully, through dialogue we will continue to lessen the probability of war.

The bottom line was clear: We should not expect the Chinese to be allies. This would be wishful thinking. What we can expect is neutrality and that they not be inimical to the interests of the United States. But let us continue to seek to become better friends.

"What we seek we shall find; what we flee from flees from us." (Ralph Waldo Emerson)

Sino-Vietnamese border conflicts

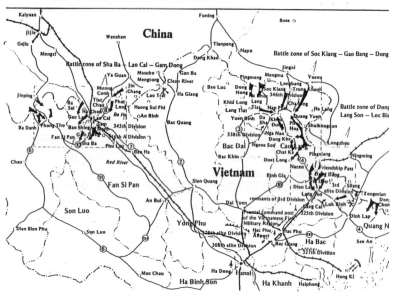

80. An Old Enemy

Throughout history, the Chinese have had conflicts with Vietnam. In 1979, when I was in Moscow, the Chinese attacked Vietnam. One of several reasons for the attack was an unwritten agreement with Thailand. During the '70s, Vietnamese were violating Thai borders, chasing Cambodian guerrillas, who fled into Thailand. The Chinese promised the Thai government that if the Vietnamese continued to violate Thai borders, China would invade Vietnam. There were several Chinese warnings. The Vietnamese disregarded them.

The Chinese invaded, sending more than 35 divisions across the entire northern border of Vietnam. Mr. Brezhnev, the Secretary General of the Soviet Union, warned the Chinese that if they did not withdraw from Vietnam immediately, there would be grave consequences. Most of us in Moscow expected the Soviets to take some action, such as mass troops or flight intrusions along the border, but nothing happened. The Chinese continued the offensive, and the Soviets continued their warnings.

It was obvious that the Russians were not ready to fight Chinese over Vietnam. There were also weaknesses in Soviet positions in the Far East. The Trans-Siberian railroad ran parallel to the Chinese border and could easily be attacked by Chinese artillery. This was one of the reasons that the late Soviet Union was building another railroad that was a thousand kilometers north of the border.

"Only the dead have seen the end of war." (Plato)

The President of the United States of America

and Mrs. Reagan

request the pleasure of your company

at dinner

on Saturday evening, April 28, 1984

at seven o'clock

Great Wall Hotel
Beijing, China

81. REAGAN'S DINNER

President Reagan was in the PRC on his first state visit. Tensions between China and Vietnam had been increasing. Shootings across the border were occurring regularly. On the Cambodian Thai border, the Cambodian Army, supported by Vietnamese troops, was chasing Cambodian rebels across the borders.

President Reagan was at a dinner, ready to deliver his final speech in China. It would stress mutual cooperation and friendship. I was seated between the Chinese Minister of Defense and Bud McFarland, Assistant to the President for National Security Affairs. At one point, the Chinese Minister of Defense turned to me, and said, "Tomorrow, we will teach Vietnam a lesson." "Could you be more specific?" I asked. "Tomorrow, you will see," answered the Minister.

I mentioned to Bud that the Minister was trying to alert us to another offensive. Bud asked one of his assistants to check out if there was anything unusual happening. A call was immediately made through the White House Communication network. Report came back of heavy Chinese movement all along the border. Bud was furious: "How could they be doing this with the President here!"

The President was to give his speech in ten minutes. Bud went over to the President's table, where a short conversation took place. Bud came back visibly shaken. It was too late to change the speech. The President read his prepared "nice" remarks. But, for the Chinese, it was time to act. What better time than during the American President's visit? Chinese troops struck across the Sino-Viet border during Reagan's Farewell Dinner. The Chinese had made it appear that, as a minimum, the U.S. had given approval to the operation. At least the Thai appreciated what the Chinese had done.

"A man cannot be said to succeed in this life who does not satisfy one friend."
(Henry David Thoreau)

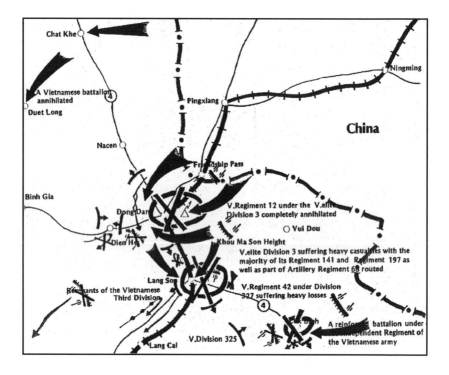

Chat Khe

A Vietnamese battalion annihilated
Duet Long

Nacen

Binh Gia

Dong Dan

Dien H

Remnants of the Vietnamese Third Division

Lang Cai

Pingxiang

Ningming

China

Friendship Pass

V.Regiment 12 under the V.elite Division 3 completely annihilated

Vui Dou

Khou Ma Son Height

V.elite Division 3 suffering heavy casualties with the majority of its Regiment 141 and Regiment 197 as well as part of Artillery Regiment 68 routed

Lang Son

V.Regiment 42 under Division 327 suffering heavy losses

V.Division 325

A reinforced battalion under Independent Regiment of the Vietnamese army

166

82. Someone was Taught a Lesson

The Vietnam incursion in 1979 ruined the already bad relations between China and the USSR. It also revealed the weakness of the Chinese Armed Forces. In three weeks, China suffered more than 20,000 troops killed. In contrast, the U.S. lost 50,000 killed in 14 years of war against the North Vietnamese. The Chinese attacked across a large border. They informed the Soviets that their purpose was to teach the Vietnamese a lesson, and said that they would soon withdraw. Coordinated attacks were few after the initial days. It was not uncommon for Chinese troops to be disoriented, since many units did not have maps of the area or sufficient compasses. No air support was used because of fear of Vietnamese air defenses and Soviet aircraft.

The casualties among officers were high. Without rank insignia, soldiers could not identify new leaders who were replacing the wounded or killed. The Chinese defend the tactics they used, stating that this was not a war in the classical sense. They maintain that this war was fought to teach the lesson that every inch of Vietnamese soil could be violated if the Chinese chose to do so. The Vietnam war influenced today's modernization of the Chinese Army to include rank insignia for their leaders.

"It's not a man's great frame or breadth of shoulders that makes his manhood count. A man of sense has always the advantage." (Sophocles)

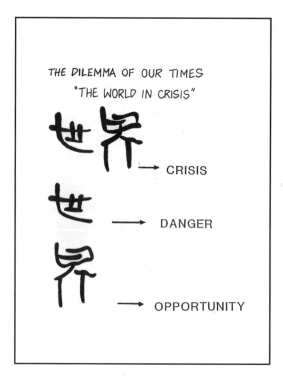

83. THE FOUR MODERNIZATIONS

During the 1980s, the leader of China was Deng Xiao Ping. One of his famous sayings was "It does not matter the color of the cat, as long as it catches mice." It was obvious to Mr. Deng that drastic steps were needed to modernize agriculture, industry, science and technology, and defense.

Mr. Deng had problems with the Chinese Army. When he chose priorities, he placed defense last, declaring that agriculture needed to be priority one. He reasoned that, "If the Chinese people are starving, they will rebel, and the Army will be fighting Chinese instead of securing borders. First priority must be to feed the nation."

He then added, "Modern industry is needed to produce equipment and consumer goods, so priority two is self-reliance in industry." Deng told the generals that he really hadn't placed defense in last priority, because focusing on the other three priorities would automatically produce a stronger defense.

Feeding the nation would free the Chinese Army from the fear of internal problems. By developing industry, the Army could rely on China to produce its own weapons. Developing science and technology would create innovations that would assist the development of agriculture, industry and defense.

Two steps forward and one back may at times be necessary to move forward.

84. If He Dies, I Will Send You Another General

For almost two years, I had been trying to become a Chinese paratrooper. The Chinese were reluctant to allow it for fear that I might be injured. During his visit to China, Secretary of Defense Weinberger personally asked the Chinese Minister of Defense to let me jump. The Minister of Defense replied, "What happens if he gets hurt or killed?" Mr. Weinberger answered, "Don't worry, I have plenty of generals in the Pentagon. I will send you another one." The Minister of Defense laughed, and within three weeks I was a Chinese paratrooper.

Being the first Westerner to jump with a regular Chinese communist parachute unit opened doors that had previously been closed. Sharing danger strengthens relationships.

───────────────

"First say to yourself what you would be, and then do what you have to do." (Epictetus)

85. It is Hard to Properly Breathe or Die in Tibet

In the early 1980s, travel to Tibet was difficult. Because Chinese authorities restricted entry into this exotic land, very few of us made the trip, and only after a rigorous Chinese medical examination.

The altitude in Lhasa, the Tibetan capital, is 12,000 feet, and it is difficult to breathe if one is not used to thin air. Tibetan medical authorities claim that it takes six months before acclimatization occurs. Those who arrive in winter have more difficulties because of less oxygen available in cold weather. In this altitude, running a seven and one-half minute mile becomes an eleven-minute mile with the same amount of exertion. During my first night in Tibet, I woke up several times gasping for air. Fortunately, the hotel rooms were equipped with oxygen bottles.

Extended exposure to high altitudes was said to be harmful. After a year and a half, Chinese assigned to Lhasa are transported to the lowlands, where they stay for three months before returning to Lhasa.

The most common diseases in Tibet are gastric ulcers and high blood pressure. The causes for gastric ulcers are a combination of eating raw meat, hot peppers, drinking barley wine, and the altitude. The cause for high blood pressure is also attributed to the altitude.

An ancient custom, prohibited by the Chinese but practiced by Tibetans, is the method by which some Tibetans choose to dispose of their dead. Those who can afford it hire a specialist, who basically strips the body of its skin and muscle. The specialist chops all the pieces into small portions so that birds can easily eat them. The bones are crushed and burned, and again fed to the birds. Many Tibetans believe that in this way they will continue to live and fly in the bodies of birds.

"We were born with wings. Why prefer to crawl though life?" (Rumi)

CHINESE RUNNERS ARRIVING IN FT. BRAGG, NC,
AFTER RUNNING FROM SAN FRANCISCO.

86. APPLAUSE

When I first went to China in the 1970s, foreigners were rare. As we walked from one street to the next, masses of Chinese would applaud. I thought they were competing to see which street could applaud the loudest.

The Chinese did many things that deserved our applause, too. They impressed us with their ability to suffer in silence, their confidence in themselves, their respect for their elders. It was also in China that I learned to appreciate acupuncture as a way to alleviate pain.

The Chinese are now used to seeing foreigners. Since the 1980s, their applause has ceased, but interest in the United States continues. Even though we have had many problems, we are still called Mei Guo Ren (the beautiful people).

"My mother had a great deal of trouble with me, but I think she enjoyed it." (Mark Twain)

Part Six:

The Missing

JOHN F. KERRY, MASSACHUSETTS,
Chairman
THOMAS A. DASCHLE, SOUTH DAKOTA
HARRY REID, NEVADA
CHARLES S. ROBB, VIRGINIA
J. ROBERT KERREY, NEBRASKA
HERT H. KOHL, WISCONSIN

BOB SMITH, NEW HAMPSHIRE,
Vice Chairman
JOHN McCAIN, ARIZONA
HANK BROWN, COLORADO
CHUCK GRASSLEY, IOWA
NANCY LANDON KASSEBAUM, KANSAS
JESSE HELMS, NORTH CAROLINA

FRANCES A. ZWENIG, STAFF DIRECTOR
J. WILLIAM CODINHA, GENERAL COUNSEL

United States Senate

SELECT COMMITTEE ON POW/MIA AFFAIRS
WASHINGTON, DC 20510-6500

16 October 1992

Major General Bernard Loeffke
ODSPER, Task Force Russia
The Pentagon, Room 2D 677
Washington, DC 20310-0300

Dear General Loeffke:

The Senate Select Committee will hold hearings on 11 November and extends to you an invitation to appear as an important witness, one who can assist us in placing in historical perspective the entire matter of unreturned American POWs from at least three wars in this century. The hearings will take place in Senate Hart 216 and will begin at 9:30 am.

We anticipate that you will appear as a member of a panel that will discuss, primarily, POWs in World War II, Korea and the Cold War, and the matter of American POWs held in the former Soviet Union and possibly transferred there from Indochina. Your panel will probably present testimony in the afternoon of 11 November; we will communicate with you more precise details later in the month.

Our rules (which are enclosed) require that the Committee be supplied with 40 copies of your testimony 48 hours in advance of your appearance. Please provide also a copy of your biography. You will be invited to make an opening statement, and we ask that it be no longer than five minutes.

If there are any questions about the hearings, please call the Select Committee Staff Director, Frances A. Zwenig, at (202) 224-2306. We look forward to your testimony in this important aspect of our investigation.

Sincerely,

Bob Smith
Vice Chairman

John F. Kerry
Chairman

JFK/kb

176

87. Where Are They?

We have 87, 000 service members unaccounted for from WW II, 7,800 from the Korean conflict, 2,200 from Vietnam, and more than 90 from ten reconnaissance flights that disappeared around the borders of the late Soviet Union.

In 1992, I became the U.S. Military's Representative to Russia, with the mission of locating our missing in action. This experience was very different from the one I had some 16 years before in Russia. We were now cooperating in many areas.

This new Russia continued to be an enigma. There is not one Russia: there are many "Russias" layered on top of each other, bumping against each other, intermingling, and sometimes struggling against each other. I am always wary of anyone who proclaims that Russia fits into one mold or another. For virtually every conclusion I have drawn about Russia in the past, I eventually found contradictory evidence.

Russia is rich and painfully poor, ingenious, creative and exasperatingly inept. I count some Russians—former enemies of my country— among my friends today, while there are others I have yet not learned to trust. I admire the courage and honor of certain Russians, even as I have had to deal with the duplicity of others. Russia is a vision that is always just receding, so enormous it is impossible to take in at a single glance. If Western experts on Russia often take positions diametrically opposed to one another, I have learned to accept the fact that each expert may be right according to his or her experience.

"Russia is a riddle wrapped in mystery inside an enigma." (Winston Churchill, in a radio address, 1 Oct 1939)

THE MAIN DIRECTORATE OF BORDER TROOPS OF THE KGB
OF THE COUNCIL OF MINISTERS OF THE USSR

(SECRET - 28 June 58)

A border detail from Outpost No. 12 of the 40th Border Detachment, Armenian Okrug spotted an aircraft approaching the border from Turkey at an altitude of 4,500 meters at 1825 hrs. on 27 Jun. The aircraft violated the State border of the USSR in the ADA-Ehri area.

Two Air Force fighters were sent up and forced the four-engine "Douglas-118" American military transport aircraft to land at 1857 hrs. in the Agdam area. The crew, consisting of four American servicemen, rushed out of the burning plane.

Five parachutists, who jumped prior to the plane's landing, were arrested in the Agdam area. All of the detainees were taken to Korovabad in the Azerbajdzhan SSR. The U.S. military personnel are: COL BRENAN BRAZH, aircraft commander, MAJ LAJZ, MAJ KREND, MAJ SHUL'TS, CPT KEJN, LT LYURER, SGT OL'MAN, SGT RIMER, SGT SEJPO.

Based on initial crew testimony, the aircraft crew flew on the route: Nikoziya (Kipr Island) [Nicosia, Cyprus], Teheran, Karachi. They strayed from their route, however, and violated the State border of the USSR.

According to their testimony, only the aforementioned crew was on the aircraft. Search groups, in conjunction with organs of the KGB, are conducting an inspection of the areas along the aircraft's flight route and in the landing area.

CHIEF OF STAFF, GUPV OF THE KGB
OF THE COUNCIL OF MINISTERS OF THE USSR
General-Lieutenant

88. What About Nuclear Weapons?

We had difficulty in getting many Russians interested in discussing the fate of American soldiers. Millions of Russians are missing inside Russia. Enormous economic problems and territorial disputes are just two of the many serious challenges they face. A subject they were eager to discuss, however, was nuclear weapons.

The Chernobyl Nuclear Plant accident exploded many illusions held by Russian military men and civilians about nuclear weapons. The accident demonstrated the impossibility of surviving a nuclear attack. In May 1993, I met a Russian general who was dying of cancer as a consequence of his participation in rescue operations during the Chernobyl incident. He told me that many of his soldiers had also been stricken with cancer.

During a conference, I sat next to a Russian parliamentarian responsible for defense matters. When asked what his top priority would be if he were to become Defense Minister, he answered without hesitation, "Nuclear weapons." He went on to say that the problem of nuclear weapons is foremost in the minds of many Russian strategic thinkers, specifically how these weapons can be effectively controlled and how nuclear war can be prevented. The nuclear issue is not one-sided. While addressing the graduating class at a high-level Russian academy, I mentioned that the Russians still have the nuclear capability to destroy us in thirty minutes or less. A Russian colonel responded, "And so do you, General, so do you." We have to be imaginative to live in harmony.

"If you don't daydream and plan things out in your imagination, you never get there. You have to start someplace." (Robert Duvall)

179

We have met Them and they are sort of like us.

89. WHICH SYSTEM IS BETTER?

On a trip to the new Russia, I made history. I lectured at the Frunze Military Academy, which is the equivalent of our Staff College, where our future Generals are trained. This would be the last graduating class that was composed of officers from all of the nations of the former Soviet Union. I was reminded of the last West Point class before our Civil War. When that class graduated, part went to fight with the South and part stayed to fight with the North.

There was tension in the air when an officer from the soon-to-secede Belorussian Republic asked, "Which system is better, the Russian multi-year Frunze Academy system or your nine-month course at Fort Leavenworth?" I answered that, for us, the nine-month course was preferable, because we could not afford to keep our officers away from the practical world for a longer time. The officer quickly replied, "The American system is better!" One of his Russian classmates told him to sit down, but the Belorussian would not relinquish the floor. Hopefully, time may lessen these tensions.

"Let us not give up meeting together, as some men are in the habit of doing, but let us encourage one another." (Hebrews 10:25)

90. Send More Sergeants

Americans and Russians share an expansiveness of both spirit and native land. There seems to be a special bond between us, yet it is not a bond so strong that it cannot be broken. We must do as much as we can to strengthen this bond, to disarm Russian insecurities, and to develop mutual understanding.

In my service on four continents, I have found that there is no substitute for personal diplomacy and for broad and repeated human contacts in building trust. Personal relationships can create mutually beneficial strategies. We need to spend a lot more time with the Russians, and to give their young officers and officials, their students and professionals, many more opportunities to see us and our country up close. The most powerful tool I know for peace and understanding is direct human contact.

A Russian admiral gave me evidence of this. During an informal, after-hours social event following a conference, I brought him together with a U.S. sergeant. The Russian's image of the American sergeant was vintage Hollywood—vulgar, rude, uneducated. But the sergeant with whom the admiral spoke for almost two hours was well-educated, articulate, professional and dedicated to the Army and to caring for soldiers.

Speaking alone with the admiral afterward, I became convinced that this single meeting had changed the admiral's perceptions. It definitely made him realize how badly the lack of professional sergeants hurts his own military establishment. He told me, "If we had sergeants like yours, we wouldn't need young officers like ours." Perhaps, in the course of the multiplying exchanges with the Russians, we should send fewer generals and more sergeants.

"Wisdom is better than weapons of war." (Ecclesiastes 9:18)

Gen. Volkogonov

91. Search for the Missing

The Army called me back from retirement in 1992 to direct Task Force Russia. Our mission: Work with the Russians to seek answers to the many questions concerning our missing in action.

After a year on the job, I was asked to report to Congress alongside my Russian counterpart, General Dimitri Volkogonov, who became the first Russian to swear to "tell the truth and nothing but the truth, so help me God." I followed General Volkogonov's testimony, and described our successes and challenges. When I had concluded, a senator asked, "Are the Russians lying to you?" I responded, "Some are very courageously telling us the truth, even though it may cost them their pensions and even put them at risk. Others continue to be less than truthful."

General Volkogonov was criticized by his country for discrediting Stalin, Lenin and telling in book form the truth about Russian communism. He was a brave man who was dying of cancer and wanted to be remembered as having told the truth.

"To thine own self be true. And it must follow as the night the day, thou canst not then be false to any man." (William Shakespeare)

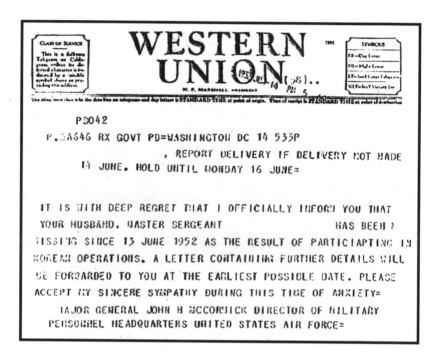

WESTERN UNION

1201

CLASS OF SERVICE

This is a full-rate Telegram or Cablegram unless its deferred character is indicated by a suitable symbol above or preceding the address.

W. P. MARSHALL, PRESIDENT

SYMBOLS

DL—Day Letter
NL—Night Letter
LT—Int'l Letter Telegram
VLT—Int'l Victory Ltr

The filing time shown in the date line on telegrams and day letters is STANDARD TIME at point of origin. Time of receipt is STANDARD TIME at point of destination.

```
P3042
P.DA646 RX GOVT PD=WASHINGTON DC 14 533P
                       , REPORT DELIVERY IF DELIVERY NOT MADE
14 JUNE. HOLD UNTIL MONDAY 16 JUNE=


IT IS WITH DEEP REGRET THAT I OFFICIALLY INFORM YOU THAT
YOUR HUSBAND, MASTER SERGEANT           HAS BEEN
MISSING SINCE 13 JUNE 1952 AS THE RESULT OF PARTICIAPTING IN
KOREAN OPERATIONS. A LETTER CONTAINING FURTHER DETAILS WILL
BE FORWARDED TO YOU AT THE EARLIEST POSSIBLE DATE. PLEASE
ACCEPT MY SINCERE SYMPATHY DURING THIS TIME OF ANXIETY=
  MAJOR GENERAL JOHN H MCCORMICK DIRECTOR OF MILITARY
PERSONNEL HEADQUARTERS UNITED STATES AIR FORCE=
```

92. COLD WARRIORS

During the Cold War, U.S. Navy and Air Force planes flew thousands of secret intelligence flights against the Soviet Union. Some consisted of electronic/signals intelligence gathering. Others were flights to probe Soviet air defenses.

These flights were dangerous, some penetrating Soviet airspace. Many of them were shadowed by Soviet planes to intimidate the crews and to track their flight paths. Ten flights were shot down between 1950 and 1965.

Some of the crew members of these ten shoot-downs were captured alive by the Soviets, survived custody, and were returned to the United States. A number were killed outright. Of these, some remains were returned to the U.S. by the Soviets. Over the years, sightings of survivors have been reported at various locations throughout the Soviet Union. They have never been confirmed. The agony of the families of these missing Americans continues.

"O my son Absalom, my son, my son Absalom! Would God I had died for thee." (Samuel 18:33)

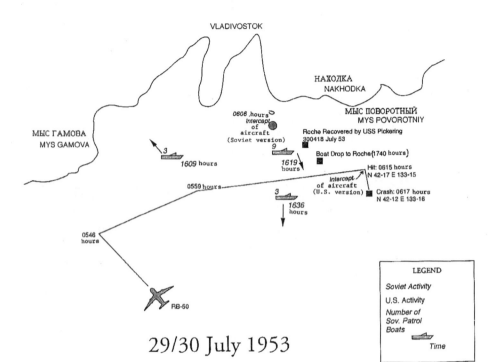

VLADIVOSTOK

НАХОДКА
NAKHODKA

МЫС ПОВОРОТНЫЙ
MYS POVOROTNIY

0606 .hours
Intercept
of
aircraft
(Soviet version)

Roche Recovered by USS Pickering
300418 July 53

МЫС ГАМОВА
MYS GAMOVA

3
1609 hours

9
1619
hours

Boat Drop to Roche (1740 hours)

Hit: 0615 hours
N 42-17 E 133-15

0559 hours

Intercept
of aircraft
(U.S. version)

Crash: 0617 hours
N 42-12 E 133-16

3
1636
hours

0546
hours

RB-50

29/30 July 1953

LEGEND

Soviet Activity

U.S. Activity

*Number of
Sov. Patrol
Boats*

Time

188

93. THE SANDERSON CASE

For more than a year, we presented evidence that led us to believe that the Russians knew more about the fate of our reconnaissance flights than they were admitting. We made the centerpiece of our presentations the case of a reconnaissance flight that was shot down in July 1953, one day after the Armistice was signed in Korea.

The flight had not checked in at the agreed time. In fact, it had missed two communication call-ins, yet the officer on duty was not overly concerned. There was bad weather, and it was not unusual for flights to have communications problems. The mood was confident: surely, nothing would happen now that the Armistice had been signed. The Soviets would certainly not harass our planes now that we were talking peace in Korea.

But this was not the case. The American plane had been shot down, and negotiations that would last for more than 40 years were about to begin.

"The relationship between man and man is bad because the relationship between man and his God is bad." (General Vessey, ex-chairman, Joint Chiefs of Staff)

94. Testifying Before Congress

1992. We did much in that one year. We had an office in Washington with analysts, translators, and computer experts. In Moscow, we had eight personnel. We pursued all leads, and we published a bi-weekly, unclassified report.

From 1977-79, little was opened to us. In the new Russia, although we were allowed limited access to archives and Russians, there were still problems. The archives that might contain information on U.S. POWs were still not available to us. We worked with the Russians, which had both positive and negative aspects. As positives, the Russians knew exactly what we were doing, we shared what we found with them, and Task Force Russia became a model of how to work with the Russians. As negative, some Russian citizens were uncomfortable having Russian officials present when they divulged information to us.

A Russian parliamentarian, Yuri Smernov, was chairman of the POW/MIA committee for the Russian parliament. It was a committee of one. Smernov was also founder of Iskatel (The Searchers), an organization of 40,000 volunteers who searched for missing Russians. General Volkogonov's father is one of a million and a half Russians who are missing.

In a Siberian town, I saw 20,000 files of Russians who were executed in the 1930s. They did terrible things to themselves. However, the archives had nothing about American POWs.

Bruce Sanderson, whose father was shot down on the day Bruce was born, met with me and General Volkogonov in Moscow. Bruce asked about his father for almost an hour. When he had finished, I said to General Volkogonov, "What have we not asked that you would have asked if you were sitting in Bruce Sanderson's chair?" The General replied, "I think you've asked all the questions. I look at Bruce Sanderson, and I see myself, because my father is also missing."

If I turn up missing tomorrow, I hope that my children will do as much for me as the Sandersons did for their father, and I hope that any wife would do as much as Jane Reynolds or Pat Service.

191

to comrade L.I. Brezhnev

MAIN INTELLIGENCE DIRECTORATE OF THE GENERAL STAFF
ENCODED TELEGRAM № 13987

TOP SECRET

Copy № 1	BREZHNEV	Copy № 9	SUSLOV	Copy № 17	RASHIDOV
" № 2	VORONOV	" № 10	SHVERNIK	" № 18	USTINOV
" № 3	KIRILENKO	" № 11	SHELEPIN	" № 19	TsK KPSS
" № 4	KOSYGIN	" № 12	SHELEST	" № 20	KUZNETSOV
" № 5	MAZUROV	" № 13	GRISHIN	" № 21	
" № 6	MIKOYAN	" № 14	DEMICHEV	" № 22	
" № 7	PODGORNIJ	" № 15	EFREMOV	" № 23	
" № 8	POLYANSKIJ	" № 16	MZHAVANADZE	" № 24	

from __HANOI__ received __1650 hrs 26 Jul 65__ copy № __1__

Subject to return to TsK KPSS   EXTRAORDINARY
(General Department, 4th sector)
Entry № 10560 shsh from 31 Jul 65

to MARSHAL OF THE SOVIET UNION COMRADE ZAKHAROV,
MARSHAL OF THE AIR FORCE COMRADE SUDETS

I am reporting:
The 4th battalion 1st SAM regiment shot down
two planes in the Sontay area (45 kilometers
west of Hanoi) on 26 Jul: one U-2 at 19000
meters,and the second currently unidentified.
Three rockets expended. The commander of the
missile battalion is Major Il'inykh.
Concurrently, I report: according to more
specific information, on 24 July, three F-
4C's were shot down; one of which crashed
(burned) and was inspected by us; the second
crashed in the jungle (pilot was captured);
the third fell in Laos, according to
intelligence information.

                    GENERAL-MAJOR IVANOV
                    (VAT [Military Attache] in DRV)

№   495
26 Jul

As these documents show, the Soviets have shot at our planes both
from the air and from the ground. These incidents occured
from the '50s to the '80s.

95. The Russians in Vietnam

The Vietnam conflict was one of our longest, most unpopular wars, lasting from 1959 through the early 1970s. We fought far from home, without solid support from our allies and with heavy opposition from the majority of the U.S. population. On the other hand, our enemy, North Vietnam, had strong support from the Soviet, Chinese and North Korean governments.

The Soviets in particular provided a great deal of technical as well as troop support. Their air defense batteries were heavily engaged in shooting down our aircraft. A top secret document retrieved from Russian archives in the '90s reveals the extent of Soviet involvement against us. The document, a report written by the Soviet General in Vietnam, details the results of Soviet air defense batteries on 26 July 1965. According to this report, Soviet misslemen assigned in Vietnam were responsible for shooting down a total of four U.S. aircraft. At least one U.S. airman was captured on that date. Officially, the Soviets denied their participation for many years.

I find it especially interesting that as we moved toward the 1980s, former allies became enemies. In 1979, the Communist Chinese invaded Vietnam, while the Soviets came to aid the Vietnamese. It was the fear of Soviet aircraft and air defense that caused the Chinese to refrain from using their aircraft in their Vietnamese offensive.

"If more grownups would do more good, our generation would have fewer wrongs to fix." (An eighth grade student)

THE WHITE HOUSE

WASHINGTON

July 2, 1993

MG Bernard Loeffke, USA
5180 Edgebaston Drive
Kernersville, North Carolina   27284

Dear General Loeffke:

I am pleased to extend my sincere appreciation for your endeavors in behalf of POWs/MIAs and their families. Your leadership as the Director of Task Force Russia and as key advisor to the special United States Ambassador serving on the Joint U.S.- Russia Commission on POWs/MIAs has been invaluable in allowing us to meet our commitment to determine the status of missing servicemen lost during World War II through the end of the Cold War.

Your rapport with your Russian counterparts enabled the commission to make significant gains in locating and analyzing information about the status of missing personnel. Your dedication earned the commission the trust and respect of the families of the missing POWs and MIAs, as well as the members of Congress who are studying these difficult issues.

I know that your counsel and devotion to duty will be missed by all who have been touched by your work. Thank you for your continuing commitment and dedication to service.

Sincerely,

Bill Clinton

96. What Do We Do Now?

I have found Russian military officers to be honorable men. Where we have learned bits of the truth about our missing service members, those shreds of evidence, documentary or from memory, usually came from serving officers or retired veterans. I believe those officers are willing to help us because we are brothers-in-arms and fellow officers, and also because the military has relatively little to hide. I am convinced that the information we seek from Korea, the Cold War or Vietnam lies in the files, safes and vaults of the successor organizations of the KGB.

In my presentations to the Russian military, I stressed that one of the most respected and loved generals in the U.S. Army was General Vessey, who had held ranks from Private to General. I told my Russian colleagues that General Vessey counseled us that it was hard to be a good soldier in the U.S. Army, but harder to be a good soldier in the Army of the Lord, as the standards were harder to meet. In the end, it may be those Russians who possess spiritual and moral values who will give us the answers we seek.

It was my privilege to work with outstanding soldiers, sailors, airmen and civilians in the pursuit of a cause as noble as any I have ever served. We searched for our lost comrades-in-arms, both for their own sakes and for the sakes of their loved ones left behind, many of whom have kept the faith for 40 years or longer. The dedication, devotion and, ultimately, the generosity of the POW/MIA family members have been an inspiration. I regret that we were not able to do even more to provide them the answers they deserve.

"In hope we were saved. Now hope that is seen is not hope. For who hopes for what is seen? But if we hope for what we do not see, we wait for it with patience." (Romans 8:24-25)

195

PART SEVEN:

A FAREWELL AND NEW BEGINNING

97. KEEP YOUR UNIFORM

I served 36 years in the Army. It went by too quickly. I taught, I fought, I bled, I spied, I cried, I laughed and at the end I left reluctantly, wishing that I could start all over again. A famous General who influenced many of us said it eloquently:

> "Don't be in a hurry to get out of uniform. Next to serving God, I have found serving country to be the noblest pursuit of man. This serving one's fellow man is what separates us from the beast. Because we are so poorly paid, meanly treated and quickly forgotten, the profession of arms must be the most unselfish in the world. Yet, in what other role can a man spend his life with greater satisfaction—serving his country in order that happiness might be pursued by neighbors he doesn't even know. In what other profession could an ordinary lad like me have been able to so serve his country and yet thrill to the challenge of the call to the most exciting tasks man can be assigned—to explore, to teach, to minister, to fight, to doctor, to spy, to judge, to lead... in the name of God and the U.S.A."

> General Douglas MacArthur

"One other thing stirs me when I look back at my youthful days. The fact that so many people gave me something or were something to me without knowing it." (Albert Schweitzer)

98. A New Career: From High Tech to High Touch

In 1997, I began a new career. After retirement from the Army, I threw myself into the study of medicine. After four years, I graduated, passed my boards, and became a certified physician's assistant. I am now able to diagnose, treat, prescribe medication and perform minor surgical procedures. It has long been my dream to be a healer. The dream has now become a reality.

This new skill has allowed me to work in space medicine, and to learn how we plan to make the two-year trip to Mars and back. Plants will provide oxygen as well as food. Space technology has also given us the GPS (Global Positioning System), a hand-held instrument that tells your location anywhere in the world.

Near the end of 1997, I was recruited to work in Sudan by Samaritan Purse. This is an organization led by Billy Graham's son, Franklin, and its mission is to populate jungle clinics with U.S. medical personnel. I was part of a three-person team consisting of a surgeon, nurse and physician's assistant. Interestingly, it was the GPS that allowed us to land our airplane in a jungle strip without the aid of any other navigational system.

After arriving in Southern Sudan, we were quickly immersed in a primitive environment. There was no electricity and no running water (unless you count Africans running with buckets). There were no x-ray machines or laboratories. Surgery was done by flashlight with reused gloves and syringes. We saw all the diseases of biblical times. We brought very little with us in material goods, but the Africans believed we brought a lot. They thought we brought miracles. We called it hope. We came in as plumbers of the body, and hoped to also be healers of the soul. I left the miracles to others. For me, plumbing is easier than preaching.

Many of the patients we treated seemed hopeless. It seems certain to me that they weren't saved by our procedures as much as by their faith in the American healers—more testimony to the mind's tremendous power. We thought our prayers may have had something to do with it, as well.

During my time in the Sudan, I was moved by three things: The experience of seeing the sick become well through faith, by meeting incredible people like the missionary pilots who fly into combat zones unarmed and in flimsy aircraft, and by rereading parts of the Bible.

"Whom shall we send?...send me." (Isaiah 6:8)

99. Franklin's List

My last story is about a simple, effective method I use to evaluate myself and my children, based on one used by Benjamin Franklin. Franklin was a great believer in personal development, and thought that everyone needed self-evaluation. Every day, he evaluated his own progress by means of a checklist. He focused on two qualities each week. Each evening, he would check off the attributes that needed improvement. Franklin felt that insufficient humility was one of his weak points. Whenever a week went by and he noticed that he had no check marks next to humility, he felt proud of being so humble, and had to check the humility box once again.

My experience as a pilot has taught me that checklists can be valuable tools. I offer my own version of Mr. Franklin's list.

	Sun	Mon	Tue	Wed	Thu	Fri	Sat
1. **Humility:** Did I conduct myself without pretentiousness or feelings of superiority?							
2. **Charity:** Did I give my time, talents, skills or resources to someone or something unselfishly?							
3. **Cleanliness:** Was I neat, well organized and orderly?							
4. **Silence:** Did I engage in trivial conversation? Did I listen attentively to what others have to say?							
5. **Perseverance:** Did I steadily work toward achieving my goals?							
6. **Fairness:** Did I treat others fairly, without bias or prejudice?							
7. **Frugality:** Did I waste resources or purchase unnecessary things?							
8. **Moderation:** Did I overeat, overdrink or overdo anything?							
9. **Sincerity:** Did my words and actions accurately reflect my beliefs and values?							
10. **Tranquillity:** Was I disturbed by trifles? Did I make time for reflection, prayer, meditation, solitude?							
11. **Thoughtfulness:** Did I consider other people's feelings before my own?							
12. **Cheerfulness:** Did I think positively, smile, and project optimism and good cheer?							

"As we have opportunity, let us do good to all people." (Galatians 6:10)

Afterword

To Marc and Kristin

As you have read, most of my life was spent in uniform preparing to
fight, fighting, or trying to prevent a fight. After Larry Morford's death
in 1970, my life was changed. I tried to learn how to prevent conflicts,
big and small. Someone once said that our generation had to study
history, strategy and the use of arms, so that you, our children, could
study art, music, dance and philosophy. We haven't yet learned how to
live peacefully as individuals, groups and nations, so some of your generation will have to continue studying strategy and the use of arms.
When I become discouraged, I focus on helping one person at a time. I
remember the good Samaritan. He helped one. If we all helped one, it
would soon add up.

You have been a strong influence in my efforts to be a better leader. You were always watching and copying what you saw. I remember two incidents with you, Marc, and one with you, Kristin:

Marc, one Sunday morning when you were four, you had jumped onto our bed and started tugging at the cross that I wear around my neck. You whispered, "Dad, you are a Jesus man." When I asked why you said that, you answered, "You wear His cross." You reminded me, without having to say anything else, that I should be doing much more to deserve being called a "Jesus man." The second incident was when you had turned five, and met a ten-year-old on the playground who pushed you to the ground. You had gone to karate school when you were three-and-a-half, but decided to quit after six months because you thought you had learned all you needed to learn. When you got up from the ground, you went over to the ten-year-old and did your karate thing, only to be thrown down again. You got up, tried it once more, and were thrown down once again. As you were getting up you turned to me and yelled, "Daddy, it isn't working!" I said, "Son, you quit your karate lessons too soon. Now go and shake that boy's hand, since he has just given you the encouragement to study more." And you did. Learning is a life-long process.

Kristin, you taught me that we should express love, even if we think we aren't being heard. I had slipped into your room early one morning. You were still asleep. I leaned over and kissed you and whispered softly, "I love you sweetheart." I started to walk out of the room, when you whispered, "I love you, too, Daddy." You made my day. Love is amazingly powerful.

As you begin to think about what to do with your lives, remember how Mother Teresa explained our purpose on earth:

"At the end of our lives, we will not be judged by how many diplomas we have received, how much money we have made or how many great things we have done. We will be judged by, 'I was hungry and you gave me to eat. I was naked and you clothed me. I was homeless and you took me in.'"

Love, Dad

Printed in the USA by Thomson-Shore.
Designed by Richard Murdoch and Hayes McNeill
and set in Bodoni MT Book by M & M Scriveners
Winston Salem, NC.